THE RECTORY MICE

'German flying machines,' said Grandfather Mouse. 'They call them zeppelins. It's the name of the man who invented them, Count Zeppelin. They're a kind of balloon, like those the children have at their parties. But these are enormously big and filled with a special gas in big containers inside a wooden framework like a flying greenhouse. And they carry a crew of soldiers with guns and bombs.'

'You mean the Germans have sent a flying machine to attack us here in Norfolk,' said Michaelmas. 'It sounds incredible.'

'The war has really begun,' said Grandfather Mouse quietly. 'And Tamburlaine is the first English mouse to have seen a real live German aviator. Spiked helmet and all.'

George MacBeth

THE
RECTORY MICE

SPARROW
BOOKS

A Sparrow Book
Published by Arrow Books Limited
17-21 Conway Street, London W1P 6JD

An imprint of the Hutchinson Publishing Group

London Melbourne Sydney Auckland
Johannesburg and agencies throughout the world

First published by Hutchinson 1982
Sparrow edition 1984

Made and printed in Great Britain
by Anchor Brendon Ltd.,
Tiptree, Essex

ISBN 0 09 932870 4

For Iseult

Contents

1
A Piece of News

On the morning my story begins, the mice at Oby rectory were enjoying a late breakfast in their beamed dining room above the back door bell. This bell was rung at six every day by the housemaid to make sure that the coachman and his wife were awake and up at the dairy in time for their breakfast. The mice didn't like the bell. It had an extremely loud, tolling ring, and it was prone to wake them up while they dozed over their juice. They'd been saying a hundred times that they'd have to do something about it.

'I wonder,' Amelia Mouse would say as she nibbled her Cheddar. Then she would pause.

'I wonder,' she'd continue, 'if we ought to take some steps about that bell?'

Amelia Mouse never annoyed other mice by giving orders, or even making statements. But she was very good at getting her own way by asking questions which contained suggestions. Michaelmas, her husband, was well aware of this and he was always quick to agree.

'I'll ask Uncle Trinity to help me gnaw through the rope,' he'd say, wiping his whiskers. 'In fact, I'll see if he's free today.'

Actually, Michaelmas had no intention of having the rope gnawn through. This would immediately have drawn attention to the mice, and produced a ferocious retribution, perhaps even an unleashing of the household cats across the rafters. There were subtler ways of dealing with the problem, including muffling the clapper with leaves, and one of these would no doubt in time be put into operation. But it sounded bold and military to talk of gnawing through the rope, and Michaelmas continued to do so, and to call upon the potential assistance of Uncle Trinity for the purpose.

Uncle Trinity, as he was known to all the mice, was in fact Michaelmas's brother. He lived in the southwest corner of the attic, so that he and his family were always able to enjoy the evening sun. When the mice had first come to live in the house, after a surprise harvest one year had ruined their two houses in the cornfield, the brothers had sat down and divided out the rafters between them. They were a friendly couple and it hadn't been difficult.

Later on, when Grandfather Mouse had had to vacate his manor in the hedgerow during an October thunderstorm, space had become a little more of a problem. Grandfather Mouse had lived on his own since Grandmother Mouse had died and he'd grown rather demanding and cantankerous. He had several square feet of rafters entirely to himself and a magnificent house made out of biscuit tins, but his belongings always tended to expand.

On the morning we're concerned with, Grandfather Mouse had dropped in for breakfast. He often did this, without warning, and Amelia Mouse was forced to keep an extra stock of cheese straws to satisfy his voracious appetite.

Usually, he insisted on a plateful of these being set down for his refreshment before he'd speak a word. But today was different. Grandfather Mouse had a piece of news.

It was a piece of news, quite literally. Someone had torn it from a newspaper. It was a ragged triangle in shape, about six inches long by four inches wide and three deep. In Grandfather Mouse's claws it had evidently got a little crushed and pierced, but it was still perfectly legible when smoothed out and laid flat on the floor.

'More trouble?' asked Michaelmas, leaning over with one paw on Grandfather Mouse's shoulder.

Grandfather Mouse shook off the paw testily.

'You mark my words,' he said: 'This means more trouble than you can ever remember, my boy.'

At this, the two little mice, Boadicea and Tamburlaine, sniggered in delight. They were always particularly amused to hear their venerable father referred to by Grandfather Mouse as a boy.

'Be quiet,' said Grandfather Mouse severely. 'I want to read you the news.'

Everyone knew that this would be a slow business and they settled back as comfortably as they could while Grandfather Mouse spread the piece of news out on his lap. There was a shuffling silence while he cleared his throat and began to read.

Archduke Ferdinand Assassinated in Sarajevo, the headline said and this is exactly what Grandfather Mouse read out. Then he paused and looked around to see the effect his words had produced.

'I know what a duke is,' said Boadicea, licking her

paws. 'It's the one who has a crown of strawberry leaves. But what's an *arch* duke?'

'It means he lives in an arch, stupid,' said Tamburlaine rather truculently. 'What else could it mean?'

'He'd be rather cold in an arch,' said Boadicea in a lofty, dismissive tone. 'And he'd have to stoop, and I don't think dukes ever stoop. Arch means, I think, he was arch. And arch means . . .'

Boadicea paused for thought.

'It means rather clever and silly,' she suggested. 'A bit like Tamburlaine,' she added.

Amelia Mouse was used to what this sort of banter could lead to, so she took a firm grip on Tamburlaine by the scruff of the neck while she cuffed Boadicea lightly but sharply on the ear.

'Enough,' she said. 'That's quite enough.'

'An archduke,' said Grandfather Mouse very grandly,

'is a particularly important sort of duke. In England we don't have them.'

'Ferdinand is the archduke – or rather *was*, poor fellow – the archduke of Austria. Assassinated means that someone has killed him.'

'Like President Lincoln,' said Boadicea, who was really rather well informed for a mouse.

'Very good,' said Grandfather Mouse, 'very good indeed. Have you any double Gloucester biscuits, Amelia Mouse?'

'I know where Sarajevo is,' said Tamburlaine as he watched Grandfather Mouse putting away a hearty breakfast. 'It's in the big atlas, downstairs in the library.'

Amelia Mouse frowned and kicked Tamburlaine under the table. There were times when it was hard to decide whether he was being sarcastic or ignorant.

'Now don't be rude,' she said, just in case.

'The point is,' said Grandfather Mouse, ignoring these interruptions, 'that this assassination means there's going to be a war.'

'What kind of war?' asked Amelia Mouse doubtfully. She didn't like the idea. It immediately conjured up visions of her children ripping each other's ears off. Amelia Mouse had to spend far too much of her time licking wounds and cuffing offenders.

'I like a good war,' said Boadicea, turning a somersault. 'It keeps you warm in winter.'

Michaelmas kept silent for a moment. He always thought before he spoke and when he did speak it tended to be something worth hearing.

'You mean a war in Europe,' he said slowly. 'Will that make any difference to us here in Norfolk?'

'I tell you this,' said Grandfather Mouse. 'There won't be many kinds of foreign cheese coming in, if we have another war. There won't be any more Camembert for Christmas. Not if they have to take on staff from the Kaiser's Germany in the kitchen.'

'It may not come to that,' said Amelia Mouse soothingly. 'Let's hope it won't. Now sit up straight, Tamburlaine, and behave like a proper mouse.'

'The bell's late this morning, isn't it,' said Michaelmas.

It did feel late and the mice all listened in silence for a moment, wondering if the bell, by some sudden act of aggression, had been put out of action by the Germans.

'I'll bet there isn't a war,' said Tamburlaine.

'I'll bet there is,' said Boadicea.

But before they could decide what to bet the bell, delayed for some unknown English reason of its own, did at last begin to toll. It tolled briefly but with a huge, quivering after-resonance which seemed to make all the rafters tremble and shake.

The mice felt their teeth chatter in their heads. It seemed like an omen of trouble to come this morning.

'I wonder if we ought to do something about that bell,' said Amelia Mouse on cue.

'I'll have a word with Uncle Trinity after breakfast,' said Michaelmas.

2
A Journey in the Morning

Boadicea, as it turned out, was right and Tamburlaine was wrong. War was declared about four weeks after the Archduke Ferdinand was assassinated, exactly as Grandfather Mouse had predicted it would be.

At first, the war made very little difference to the mice in Norfolk. The cheese shortages which Grandfather Mouse had anticipated showed very few signs of happening. In fact, there was generally just as much to eat as before.

The monthly foraging expeditions to the butler's pantry were no less hazardous than usual, but the amount and variety of the cheese laid in there was as generous and mouth-watering as always. The mice continued to eat well and prosper.

The first real sign of hostilities was a surprising one, and it was young Tamburlaine who was responsible for the mice being aware of it. It happened like this.

One particular day, early in 1915, when the frost was

still hard on the molehills in the paddock, Tamburlaine decided to make a trip downstairs early in the morning. He'd woken up rather before his usual time and he lay for a while in his warm bed of straw wondering what to do. Nobody else was awake, not even Boadicea, who was normally an early riser, and Tamburlaine was bored. He knew from experience that the other mice didn't like being roused from sleep before they were ready so he decided that he would either have to go back to sleep or get up and try to amuse himself.

He tried to fall asleep again for quite a long time, squeezing his eyes tight shut and wrapping his paws round his stomach, even counting cheeses rolling out of a cheese-press, but none of this seemed to help. He was still wide awake.

There was nothing for it. He'd have to get up, as quietly as he could, and find something to do to keep himself entertained until the other mice roused from their slumbers.

With a long stretch, which uncurled him from a ball into a fur sausage, Tamburlaine worked the night stiffness out of his body and rolled onto his feet. He sniffed the air, feeling the January cold seeping in through the cracks in the roof. Then he set off along the main joists towards the chimney stack.

It had suddenly occurred to him what he could do to fill in his time. Nobody else was awake so it must be very early. That meant it would still be safe to go downstairs into the main house and look around. He'd have to be quick before the maid came down with her mop and pail to wash the hall or the odd-job boy arrived to brush the boots and shoes or wipe the cutlery in the knife-cleaning churn. But he was a quick runner and he thought he could do it.

The rules for going downstairs were very detailed and exact, and all the little mice had had them dinned into their ears since the day they were born. The main rule was that you only made your visits after midnight, when the rector and his family were in bed, or before six o'clock in the morning, when the servants rose to begin the day. The second rule was that you avoided the area beyond the green baize door, where the household cats ruled by night as well as by day.

In the event of a journey being necessary at other times it could only be made in the company of an adult and, even then, human mealtimes had to be scrupulously avoided.

The way downstairs from the attic was surprisingly simple. There was a small crack in the floor beside the main chimney breast and from this a winding route led down from brick to brick through a long tunnel just to one side of the main flue. Even when all the fires in the house were burning at full blast in mid-winter, the tunnel was still protected from the sparks and the soot. It was warm, even scorching, in places, and there were one or two port-holes with a superb view of the blaze, but in general it was a safe and comfortable route to the ground floor.

At that point it was possible to track sideways and make your way behind the skirting board in the drawing room to a point where there was a concealed opening at the top of the steps to the wine cellar. Experience had taught the mice that this was the least frequented part of the whole house, except when the rector had his port and his beer delivered.

So on this cold January morning young Tamburlaine squirmed quickly down the tunnel, scuttled along the passage behind the tall skirting board and paused for

breath in the spacious room the mice had created on their own side of the opening.

Here there were heavy chips of wood and brick, which could be pushed, if need be, across the entrance to keep out the reaching claws of the cats. There were also piles of wool and straw to rest or hide in if someone should think of shining a light into the hole. And, most important of all, there was the huge metal bath tub and the cake of Lifebuoy soap.

The bath tub had once been a baking tin, which the mice had discovered in a corner of the attic and managed, with colossal effort, to drag down the tunnel to the ground. The Lifebuoy soap had been an even more hazardous job to move. It had been slid along the hall tiles from the downstairs cloakroom when it fell one day to the floor from the hand-basin.

'You see,' Michaelmas had said, when he organized

the team to move these things, 'the rector and his family recognize us mainly by our smell. They're really not very observant with their eyes. Time and time again, it's been proved that it's their noses they use to find us out. So whenever we enter their part of the house, it's an obvious precaution to wash. All over. From head to tail. That way, they'll never notice we're here.'

This rule had become the most sacred of the lot, and it had surely saved the lives of the mice a hundred times over. It was a nuisance to take a complete bath every time you wanted to enter the house, but the mice had come to accept this as a necessary chore.

So today young Tamburlaine climbed up the half brick at the edge of the tin and slid down on his tail into the icy water. With both paws he gripped the top edge of the tin and climbed out on another brick, and then rubbed down both sides of his fur on the rounded side of the cake of soap. Then he stood up again on his hind feet and dived head first into the water.

This time it felt less cold, and he swam to and fro for a moment, enjoying the exercise, before climbing out and shaking himself dry on the bricks. To complete the process, he took a quick roll in the pile of wool in the corner which served as a towel. Tingling all over with health and feeling very clean and refreshed, he scuttled to the opening of the room and looked carefully out.

3

The Strange Little House

Ahead of Tamburlaine the hall tiles stretched bleakly and rather uninvitingly away into the distance. Tamburlaine put out a tentative foot.

'Ooh,' he said to himself, and shivered.

The tiles were icy cold. By this time in the morning, the stove under the mantelpiece had burned rather low and the fires in the other rooms hadn't yet been lit. Very soon the maid would come in with her hod of coals and her basket of sticks, but for the moment the hall was at the mid-winter of its temperature cycle.

Tamburlaine scuttled very quickly along the skirting board by the dining room, then paused and looked cautiously right and left. No one was coming. With a swift spurt, he dashed across the breadth of the hall and crouched panting for breath under the towering marble of the chimneypiece.

At his back the metal stove was a dwindling cauldron of fire, which he could see spitting and seething behind its mica doors.

It was rather dusty in the hall. There were one or two tangles of fluff as big as Tamburlaine's head and some awkward gritty lumps under his paws as he made his way, more slowly now, towards the door of the library. The maid would make short work of all this when she came down with her broom and shovel but she'd make short work of young Tamburlaine, too, if she found him. So perhaps he was lucky, after all, to have only a little soot and dust to contend with.

By the door of the library, which was tightly closed, Tamburlaine found what he was looking for, a small unobtrusive hole tucked away behind a Chinese umbrella stand. Squeezing through this, he entered a narrow corridor and rapidly made his way down until he came to a brick step and another hole which led him directly out at the side of the great walnut and rosewood bookcase.

Tamburlaine looked carefully round. Like all the mice, he had a great respect for books and the library was for him the most notable and splendid room in the house. He admired its tall, floor-length plate-glass windows which gave a beautiful prospect over open fields to the south. During the day, these windows allowed a flood of sunshine to fall in over the leather armchairs and the open family bibles.

At night, of course, the windows were covered and only tiny chinks of light would break through the gaps in the shutters.

'That's funny,' said Tamburlaine to himself.

He scratched his armpit with his paw. According to Grandfather Mouse, the shutters were always closed a little before sunset, except occasionally in summer when the windows were left open all night long to the moths and the moon.

But this was January. Tamburlaine knew that,

because it had just been his Uncle Trinity's birthday. And January was winter, everyone knew it was. You could feel January in your bones. It was a very biting month. Even the rector and his family could surely feel it was January.

So why had the shutters not been drawn?

'It's funny,' said Tamburlaine, aloud this time to reassure himself, but very quietly just in case anyone should hear him.

Normally, the shutters not being drawn would have meant that someone had risen early, the rector himself perhaps, and come down and opened them up. This would certainly be a sign of danger, and any sensible mouse would at once have scuttled back out of sight and made his way as quickly as possible upstairs again to the rafters.

But not Tamburlaine. Tamburlaine could see no sign of the rector, or any other member of the family for that matter. And he was still at the age, unfortunately, when what he couldn't see didn't worry him.

What he *could* see, moreover, represented a very strong temptation. Even in the dark the long glossy table would have been an alluring sight for the eyes of a little mouse. In the glittering light of the early morning, with a tiny splash of sun on one far corner, it was more than Tamburlaine could resist.

He just had to get up somehow and roll along the top of it. As it happened, there was an easy way this morning to do just that. If Tamburlaine had had to negotiate the brass castors, and then claw his way up a sheer face of fluted mahogany leg, he'd probably have had to give up in disgust. There would certainly have been no way he could climb over the enormous overhang where the top of the table rested on the underside. It would have daunted a full-grown rat, far more a tiny housemouse.

But there was a chair drawn up with its back close to the table, and a rolled map had been left resting against the seat of this chair. The map was a rough-looking linen one, and it seemed to offer the chance of a good grip.

'Lucky me,' said Tamburlaine and he rushed out and over the carpet, stumbling and wading in the thick felt, until he reached the point where the slanting scroll touched the ground. With teeth and claws he took a firm grasp, felt the fibres tear a little but hold, and then he was on his way, tugging and scrambling up, foot by foot, until he reached and dropped down onto the smooth green leather of the chair-seat.

Here he paused for breath. The carpet seemed a long way below, as he peered.down, and the back of the chair towered above him like a broken oak cliff, as he peered up.

Must get on, thought Tamburlaine. No time to stand and stare.

So, with a tensing of his muscles, he 'gripped the carved upright of the chair-back and started to claw his way up towards the rim of the table. It was a difficult climb, and he tried hard not to think how far it was down to the carpet and how hard the floorboards would be if he fell and landed on them.

To keep his spirits up, he sang a heroic mouse song he'd learned from his mother. Tamburlaine had a good memory for tunes, but he was bad on words. So he just hummed the melody and put in a series of tum-ti-tums, except for the bit he liked best and always did remember.

'Great mice have been before me,' sang Tamburlaine. 'Great mice are still to come. Ti-tum-ti-tum-ti-tum-ti. Ti-tum-ti-tum-ti-tum.'

It certainly sounded very well, this cold morning, up

there on the precipitous chair-back and it got him to the topmost rim without serious mishap. Once he slipped on an acorn moulding and bruised his foot. Once he lost his grip on a chipped urn and nearly fell. But he recovered his balance and at last stood, safe and sound and breathless, looking over at the dark reddish gleam of the tabletop, only a mouse-length away.

There was nothing for it now. He'd have to jump the last part of the way. Closing his eyes, Tamburlaine bunched himself up and leapt. Then he was safely over.

To his right, there was a pile of books. Behind him and to his left the table was clear, and gleamed with all the open authority and inviting smoothness he'd dreamed of.

Ahead of him, however, and almost totally blocking his view of the window, there was a surprise. Tamburlaine, as has been said already, was a very curious little mouse, and he was also a very changeable one. At the sight of this intriguing new object, all his previous interest in sliding on the tabletop was forgotten.

With a careful sliding motion, as if on skis, Tamburlaine made a sort of skating progress towards the new object. When he reached the edge of the table, it rose above him in the shape of a long tube, pointing out towards the sky and supported from below on a set of three angled legs resting on castors on the floor.

The three legs were a bit like the sort of stool the farm girls used to sit on to milk their cows, but they were much taller and somehow very much grander looking. Tamburlaine had never seen anything like them. The long tube might have been a gun and Tamburlaine knew how dangerous those could be, but he'd never before seen a gun that someone wasn't holding in his arms.

Altogether it was very strange. But the strangest and most interesting thing of all was that the long tube seemed to have a little window in it, round in shape, that was poised only an inch or two above Tamburlaine's head.

It's a little house, thought Tamburlaine, with mounting excitement. But I wonder what kind of creature can possibly live in there?

There was only one way to find out. Rude though it might be, and dangerous as it probably was, Tamburlaine decided that he'd have to take a look in through that window. What he didn't realize was that the little round port-hole wasn't, in fact, a window at all.

It was a lens. And the long, thin tube wasn't a house. It was a telescope.

4
The Monster at the Window

Very carefully, Tamburlaine raised himself on his hind
legs, and sniffed cautiously at the lower rim of the
window. It smelled cold and brassy. Tamburlaine let
himself fall back onto all fours again.

He thought for a moment, staring up at the
plasterwork acorns which formed a decorative cornice
all round the ceiling of the library. Then he lifted
himself up again and, very gingerly, touched the rim of
the window with his paw.

Hmn, yes, he thought, it *is* cold.

Tamburlaine made up his mind. He was going to
have to take his courage in both hands and grasp hold of
this long house by the edges and peer in through that
enticing little window and see just who or what was there
inside.

He took a deep breath.

'Great mice have been before me,' he hummed. 'Now
for it.'

With a quick leap, Tamburlaine seized hold of the brass rim, swung by both paws and lifted his head to peer in through the little window.

Hanging as he was, with both feet clear of the table, he didn't have much time to stare in before his arms began to ache and he wanted to let go. But it was long enough to feel an acute sense of disappointment.

There didn't seem to be anyone in the house. It seemed to be empty. All that Tamburlaine could see was a sort of white, blank space.

'How very boring,' he said to himself. 'There must be *someone* there. Perhaps I could try knocking.'

Most little mice would have regarded knocking on the door of a strange animal's house early in the morning as a rather hazardous and unwise procedure, but not Tamburlaine. Once he got an idea in his head, he was determined to work it out to its logical, even if rather perilous, conclusion.

So, taking a short run, up he leapt and beat his fist in a rapid rum-ti-tum-ti tattoo on the bottom of the leather tube. Then he walked back, stood on tiptoe again, took a grip and swung himself from the rim of the window for a second time.

At first, everything looked exactly the same. White space, with nothing in it. But, as he looked more closely, anxious as he was for someone to be there and to come out and play with him, Tamburlaine suddenly noticed a tiny, very tiny black dot in the bottom right hand corner of the window.

For as long as he could he watched this, then, when his arms grew too tired, he let go and fell back on the glossy smoothness of the tabletop.

Tamburlaine stretched himself out and flexed the muscles in his forepaws while he thought about what he'd seen. He couldn't at all make out what it might have been. It was very small, quite small enough to have been an insect, like a mite or a tiny gnat.

The odd thing was that Tamburlaine could have sworn it seemed to grow slightly bigger as he watched it. This was intriguing. But the creature in the little window was much too small to be a threat to Tamburlaine even if it got quite a lot bigger. So Tamburlaine decided to take another look at it. He clasped the rim of the window and, for a third time, hauled himself into the air.

'Wow,' he said aloud, amazed by what he saw.

He let go his grip in his surprise and fell back to the table and bruised his back. He rubbed himself to ease the pain and slid over to the pile of books to think things out.

Leaning back on the green and gold spine of *Pilgrim's Progress*, Tamburlaine rested and calmed himself. This time the dot had been many times bigger. It had had wings and a beak and a roving eye. It had looked exactly, in fact, like the sort of greeny-black sheened bird that Tamburlaine knew was called a starling.

But how could a starling have been in that little house? It didn't seem possible that there would be room for it yet it had looked as large and as clear as life, and it had appeared to stare young Tamburlaine directly in the eye.

Tamburlaine shivered. He was beginning to feel just a tiny little bit terrified and yet his curiosity was rising nearly to boiling point. For a few seconds there was a battle inside his breast between a fearful prudence and an insatiable spirit of inquiry.

The spirit of inquiry won. Shoving himself away from his tooled leather refuge, Tamburlaine skated one more

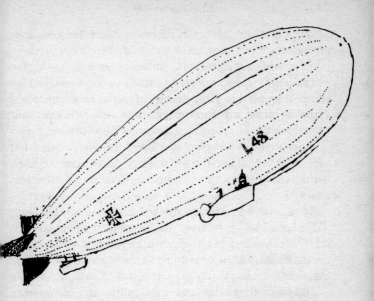

time across the polished mahogany and slithered to a stop underneath the now familiar black leather tube.

He looked up, seized hold of the window rim and dragged himself off the ground. For what seemed a kind of mouse eternity, he hung frozen to the rim of the window, quite literally rigid and motionless with fear. His paws locked on the chill brass, the fur on his neck stood on end and his dangling toes curled into thunderstruck little fists.

The round circle of the window was almost entirely filled by a gigantic silver fluted monster unlike anything Tamburlaine had ever seen or even imagined before. He'd come across pictures of fiery dragons with tails and forked tongues, but he'd never known one in real life, in the sheltered garden of Oby rectory. And he'd certainly never heard of one with three great grey ears like an elephant's and an open glittering jaw underneath like a

shark's and with a huge black crossed scar marked on its
flopping skin.

It couldn't be true. He must be still in his warm
bundle of fur, fast asleep and having a nightmare as he
sometimes did before waking up in the morning. He'd
have to make a big effort, strain to open his eyes and
then it wouldn't be there any more.

But he did, and he couldn't, and it was. And worst of
all, as Tamburlaine hung paralysed and forced to watch
whatever was going to happen, there was a face and
shoulders of a man, with a long drooping moustache
and a spiked helmet on his head, glaring straight into
Tamburlaine's eyes from the monster's open jaws.

Closer and closer the monster seemed to come. It
must be floating or swimming in some way Tamburlaine
couldn't understand. Now it almost filled the whole
window with its billowing bulk and the face of the man
was pressing forward to grind itself into poor Tamburlaine's exposed underbelly.

He felt an involuntary shudder run through his fur
and then, before he was aware of what was happening,
his paws had released their hold and he was rolling over
and over on the wonderful safe mahogany and, for the
moment, the monster had missed him in its first swoop.

Like a flash, Tamburlaine was over to the edge of the
table, had leapt, clutched, staggered, regained his
balance and was shinning down the oak chair-back as
fast as he could move. He took the length of the rolled
map in a quick slide, tumbled off onto the shag of the
carpet, fell, rose and scampered for the hole in the wall.

Terrified to look back or up, Tamburlaine squeezed
through the hole and raced along the passage behind
the skirting board. Out he came into the hall, nose first,
looking neither to right nor left. And, swoosh, he raced

across the tiles almost directly under the heels of the chambermaid who was mercifully too preoccupied in squeezing out her mop into a bucket to see him.

Pitter patter along the skirting board, scimper scamper down the corridor in the drawing room, and gasp, gasp, gasp up the twisting fiery length of the spiral past the chimney and home into the safe lofty wooden parallels of the attic rafters.

But here an outraged figure confronted him.

'Well,' said Amelia Mouse grimly. 'And where have you been at this time of the morning, young Tamburlaine?'

Even as she spoke the bell began to toll, setting the rafters quaking with its heavy ominous roll. Tamburlaine abruptly sat down, seeing his mother bending over him, knowing that he was safe and that he had a fearsome tale to tell.

He let his little head droop into his paws as the noise of the bell shook and reverberated throughout the attic. It sounded in his ears like the frustrated bellow of the monster that had failed to catch him, who would go hungry and might wait and try to find him another day. And would know his face, and would never forget his terror, and perhaps his appetizing fleshiness.

Tamburlaine burst into tears.

'I'm sorry,' he sobbed. 'But I saw a monster.'

5

The Monster's Identity Revealed

'Describe the monster,' said Grandfather Mouse in his most serious but also fairly gentle way.

The whole family of mice were gathered round to hear Tamburlaine tell his tale. Ten minutes had elapsed since his abrupt return to the rafters and his confrontation with Amelia Mouse at the hole by the chimney breast. He'd been given a big bowl of rain-water and some chunks of the very best Wensleydale, and he'd been allowed to gulp all this down, take a deep breath and lie back and rest in a pile of feathers before he began the story of his adventure.

Grandfather Mouse had been summoned from his own quarters and had been installed in his favourite corner to interpret what Tamburlaine might have to say. He didn't at first like the look of young Tamburlaine at all. He seemed to have had a very nasty fright, and

Grandfather Mouse was rather worried himself about what he might be going to hear.

'Describe the monster, young Tamburlaine,' he repeated in the same tone as before.

Tamburlaine was beginning to feel much better now that he was safely ensconced again in the midst of his family, and he paused for a moment before he started to speak. Indeed, he was just on the verge of thinking that he might have enjoyed what had happened if it was going to make the older mice pay such special attention to him.

'Well,' he said, slowly. 'The monster was in a long thin house standing on the floor of the library.'

Remembering Grandfather Mouse's prohibition about ever climbing up onto the glossy mahogany table, Tamburlaine judged that it would be best not to be too precise about where he'd been when he found the monster's house.

'Hmn,' said Grandfather Mouse thoughtfully. 'On the floor, eh? Well, it certainly wasn't there yesterday when I went down to glance into the dictionary.'

Fortunately for the education of the mice there was a low table, converted, in fact, from a commode, on which the rector sometimes left a book of reference lying open and Grandfather Mouse often took advantage of this to broaden his mind without taking the risk of pulling a volume down from the shelves. The book most frequently left open was a large, leather-bound Chambers's dictionary and pages of this were known by Grandfather Mouse almost by heart. This and the Bible, in fact, were his most revered works of literature.

'You see, it was more sort of standing up from the floor on tall legs,' said Tamburlaine, carefully.

'Standing up,' said Grandfather Mouse, who now did

the same thing himself, wrinkling his nose and rubbing his paws together. 'Now I wonder how it managed that, young Tamburlaine.'

'It had a window in it,' said Tamburlaine. 'It was through the window that I saw the monster.'

'Through the window,' said Grandfather Mouse, who was evidently beginning to see himself in the role of Sherlock Holmes as he paced to and fro, nodding his head and furrowing his brow. 'I imagine the window must have been situated at the bottom of those tall legs you mentioned.'

'Well, not exactly,' said Tamburlaine.

'He means not at all,' said Boadicea, curling her tail round her neat rump. 'He's prevaricating.'

'I'm certainly not,' said Tamburlaine, who supposed that this formidable new word meant being rude in some way, like belching. 'You're prevaricating yourself.'

'Now, children,' said Michaelmas sternly. 'Behave yourselves. And you, young Tamburlaine, just tell your grandfather what sort of thing you saw and don't be so roundabout about it.'

Actually, Grandfather Mouse wasn't best pleased by this instruction. He was rather enjoying the business of winkling out the information piece by piece. So he hurriedly put in a new suggestion to Tamburlaine.

'You must have had to climb up to reach the window,' he said. 'If the house was standing on tall legs the window was probably well above the ground.'

'As a matter of fact,' said Tamburlaine, 'it was.'

Then he took a deep breath.

'To be perfectly honest with you,' he said.

'Which you weren't being before,' said Boadicea.

Tamburlaine ignored this.

'I had to climb up onto the big library table to see,' he mumbled all in a rush.

There was an awful silence. Grandfather Mouse frowned very solemnly down at his paws.

'Tamburlaine,' he said at last. 'I made it perfectly clear, I think, that you were never, but absolutely *never*, to climb up onto that library table.'

'Oh, yes, indeed,' said Tamburlaine nodding his head. 'You made it perfectly clear. Absolutely perfectly clear. But then, you see, I did come across this tall, mysterious house, and I wanted to find out who was in it. In case it was dangerous to us all,' he added rather lamely.

Michaelmas closed his eyes and then opened them very wide so that a flash came out of them.

'You know as well as I do,' he said in a rare mood of anger, 'that any danger is to be reported to me. And *I* shall decide how to deal with it. Is that understood? Now hurry up and tell us what it was you saw.'

Tamburlaine gulped. He didn't like his father being angry. It didn't happen very often but when it did it was usually about something of real importance.

'When I got up on the table,' said Tamburlaine, 'I stood on my hind legs and looked in through this little round brass window. At first I couldn't see anything, then I looked again and I saw a dot, and then I looked again and I saw a starling.'

Grandfather Mouse and Michaelmas were exchanging relieved glances. Michaelmas looked markedly less tense.

'No doubt about it,' said Grandfather Mouse, in satisfaction. 'You've seen a telescope. I expect the rector's just bought one from the Acle sale. I remember now that he had a book about astronomy lying open on the table. He's obviously decided to start examining the night sky. That's why the library shutters were left open and you were able to see out through the main window into the air and watch a starling flying by. No reason to be afraid of a starling. But I can well see it might have given you quite a start when you weren't expecting it.'

'So much for the monster,' said Boadicea. 'It was just a silly old starling.'

'Oh, no, it wasn't,' said Tamburlaine quickly. 'I did see a starling. But I saw something else as well. Something very much nastier.'

But nobody seemed to be listening.

'It's a bit like a gun,' Grandfather Mouse was explaining to Boadicea, who'd asked what a telescope was. 'In fact, it's like a gun with lenses in it for making things look bigger when they're at a distance.'

'Like those binoculars the men carry when they go out shooting pheasant,' said Boadicea, who'd seen a pair of Zeiss glasses lying in the rector's study one day and had secretly nestled down in the gap between the tubes for a very comfortable snooze.

'Indeed so,' said Grandfather Mouse. 'Ten marks to you. But a telescope is even more powerful. It can magnify the stars in their courses.'

Tamburlaine, who'd been attending to all this with mounting annoyance, could hold himself back no longer.

'Well, maybe it magnified my monster,' he shouted, bristling his whiskers. 'But the monster was certainly there. And it wasn't a starling. It came after the starling had gone.'

At this, there was a doubtful silence. Then Grandfather Mouse turned his head and stared down at the flushed and angry Tamburlaine.

'Tell us,' he said gently. 'What was it you saw, young Tamburlaine?'

'Well,' said Tamburlaine, a little mollified. 'I saw this huge fat silver tube thing, like an . . . I don't know what.'

Tamburlaine searched his experience for a parallel to that grey flopping horror that had swum so inexorably towards him in the round glass window.

'Like an elephant,' he suggested. 'Or a sort of fish. A whale, maybe. Or a shark.'

These monsters were familiar to Tamburlaine only from the illustrations in a large children's encyclopaedia he'd found on the floor of the nursery, desecrated by crayons and scissors, but still remotely recognizable and rather terrifying.

'But worst of all,' he went on, 'the monster had a man in its mouth. A man with a droopy moustache and a helmet with a spike on his head. I only just got away before . . .'

Tamburlaine broke off and shuddered. The sense of panic he'd felt in the library returned in a sudden gush. He cowered down, shivering.

'Oh, dear,' he said. 'It was so frightening.'

Amelia Mouse lifted him up and cradled his head in her arms, rocking him to and fro for a moment to reassure him.

'You're all right now,' she said soothingly. 'We're all here to protect you.'

Grandfather Mouse was rising and stretching.

'Yes,' he said, slowly. 'It's clear enough what it was young Tamburlaine saw. They've been writing about them for several weeks in *The Times* newspaper.'

'What?' asked Boadicea. 'Monsters?'

'German flying machines,' said Grandfather Mouse. 'They call them zeppelins. It's the name of the man who invented them, Count Zeppelin. They're a kind of balloon, like those the children have at their parties. But these are enormously big and filled with a special gas in big containers inside a wooden framework like a flying greenhouse. And they carry a crew of soldiers with guns and bombs.'

'You mean the Germans have sent a flying machine to attack us here in Norfolk,' said Michaelmas. 'It sounds incredible.'

'The war has really begun,' said Grandfather Mouse quietly. 'And Tamburlaine is the first English mouse to have seen a real live German aviator. Spiked helmet and all. No wonder he was frightened.'

'Well, of course, I wasn't *really* frightened,' said Tamburlaine. 'I had a shrewd idea what it was, all the time.'

It was several days later that the mice discovered the full details. Grandfather Mouse managed to read the whole story in a copy of the *Illustrated London News*, tipped into the waste-paper basket in the maid's bedroom. The zeppelin had been over Norfolk for several hours, and had been seen heading out to sea over Yarmouth by a number of farm labourers on their way to work in the morning. The machine had arrived after dark, and had dropped a bomb in the grounds of Sandringham House. But, very fortunately, the king, though in residence, had neither been harmed nor disturbed.

The mice, loyal as they were, drank a celebratory bowl of hazel syrup and offered a prayer for the monarch's continued safety.

6
An Afternoon's Daydreaming

For some months the war continued, uneventful as before so far as the mice were concerned. There were other zeppelin raids, and casualties from them, but the placid life of Oby rectory remained undisturbed.

The first hint of a closer involvement with the business of warfare came through an unexpected visitor, and one encountered under mildly dramatic circumstances by Boadicea.

One day in spring, when the hawthorn was in blossom, Boadicea had decided to sun herself on her favourite spot in the gutter just above the front door. Towards evening, when the sun was starting to slope to the west, there was always a warm beam on this side of the house. Indoors, it fell through the sash window onto the upstairs hall, where it cast a mellow glow over the chocolate velvet of the sofa, the tooled green leather of the small writing table, and even as far as the gold-framed engraving of *Ramsgate Sands*. On the roof, it scattered a lane of brightness on the overlapping elegance of the slates, and, where those merged into the curved lead of the flashing, Boadicea had drawn together a heap of sticks and chestnut leaves to form a graceful bower.

She was a mouse with a taste for indolence and luxury, and she enjoyed nothing more than to lie in the afternoon sun here and daydream of bold rats who would carry her off to exotic foreign lands in wherries from Yarmouth or Cromer. The details of these ravishments varied, but they were always cast in the sumptuous prose of the author Ouida, whose romantic novels had crossed Boadicea's path in the carriage house, where the coachman's wife had a fine collection.

On this particular day, Boadicea had brought a few slices of preserved rose hips and she was lying with her eyes closed under a wide sycamore parasol, nibbling and dreaming of Eric. For some time, Eric had been the favourite amongst the imaginary bold rats. He had had a number of careers, all more or less criminal and magnificent, including a spell as Rat in Ordinary to the King of Prussia, a monarch who lived on hazelnuts, which Eric procured for him in enormous numbers from a wood in Silesia. This brought him jewels and power.

On another occasion, when Boadicea had been wandering in the herb garden, Eric had become a colonel of infantry in the American Civil War, and had done remarkable deeds in the service of the Union. These exploits had allowed him, as had all his others, to seek the sometimes wayward but at heart constant attentions of his lifelong sweetheart and eventual lifetime companion, Boadicea.

Honeymoons in coconut shells had alternated with

torrid affairs under draughty floorboards, but the spirit of true love had invariably transformed each encounter, whether opulent or tawdry, into the blissful substance of fantasy. Boadicea's imagination was fruitful, and it fed her appetite for romance with the heightened colours of the best modern romantic fiction.

The sun was still hot with that special May promise of strawberries to come, and Boadicea was allowing Eric an unusual privilege. He was Captain Eric today, a swashbuckling buccaneer on the Spanish Main, and his latest booty, from a sparkling raid on Guyana's Georgetown, had included the beautiful Creole maiden, Boadicea. Boadicea was about to yield him a single kiss, after a ferocious struggle, tail by lashing tail, in the alluring privacy and disorder of the Captain's cabin.

At this very moment, there was an unexpected, and rude, interruption. The background to Boadicea's reverie, as she'd been lying with eyes closed and head back on her cushion of leaves, had been the occasional flutter and cheep of a sparrow landing, or the remote swish and hush of the breeze. She'd been quite secluded, and protected from noise, in her nook in the long, grey-metal corridor of the guttering.

But suddenly, there was a difference. First of all, there was a steady deep roaring, then a sharp, high peep-peep-peep sound, then a scrunch of gravel, a louder, stilled roaring, and the sound of a door slamming. Finally, there was the dull jangle of the house's front door bell ringing.

Boadicea was brought smartly and abruptly back into the present. The startling whiskers of her delicious Captain Eric leapt back from her parting lips, and his whole incredible, oak-planked ship dissolved into English daylight. The house bell was still ringing, and the loud roar coughed into silence, as Boadicea leapt from her couch, rubbed her eyes and clambered swiftly up the sides of the guttering to peer over.

Poking her little nose between the dog-tooth patterning of the iron, Boadicea looked out to right and to left. Away on one side stretched the Portuguese laurel, with the horse chestnut beyond it, and the open fields towards Ashby Hall. On the other side, lay the gentle curve of the orchard wall, with the gothic door through it to the kitchen garden.

Nothing to be afraid of there. In front of Boadicea, and ahead, there was a swoop and dip of martins, the first volley returned from Africa, and already at work preparing the materials for their summer nest on the south of the house. Beyond them were the barns, the carriage house, and the arch of the formal garden, with its flaking urns and its decaying statue of Niobe.

Nothing to be afraid of there either. It was directly below Boadicea that the disturbance was being caused. Of course, Boadicea had already realized this, but a strict instruction from Grandfather Mouse had insisted that whenever danger threatened the young mice should test each quarter of their surroundings for signs of trouble and never jump to easy conclusions.

So Boadicea was taking care. Satisfied that she was safe on all sides, she climbed right up and looked straight down at what had arrived, with such enormous and terrifying noise, at the rector's front door.

What it was was something that she'd seen before, but not often, and never so close, and certainly never so grand and bright. It stood there on the sweep of gravel, steaming slightly under its oiled straps, the sun glittering from its polished door handles, and the hilt of its brake lever, and the grooved, enamel-tipped brass of its radiator cap.

The motorcar was quiet now, and its keeper, a very neat young officer, in puttees and cap, with a swagger stick under his arm, and a smart toothbrush moustache, was standing back from the scrubbed doorstep, waiting for his summons to be answered. As Boadicea was admiring the curled pips on his shoulder, and the sharp cut of his hair at the ears, the door opened, and the housemaid appeared, as crisp as the lace in her white apron and belt.

There was a brief exchange of words, which Boadicea couldn't quite hear, and then the housemaid was showing the young officer inside and the door was closing. There was a long hush, marked only by the resumed twitter of sparrows and an occasional creak or wheeze from the glittering machine now left on its own to wait and rest.

Boadicea looked down at the motorcar with a mixture

of emotions. She felt annoyed at having been disturbed, and at the same time a little frightened by what had disturbed her. But she was also anxious to find out what was going to happen, and why this imposing machine had come to the house. And she was still a little heady from the dazzle of the sunshine, and the aftermath of her daydreaming.

It wasn't long, as she dropped back from the parapet and stretched out in her leaves again, before the handsome young officer with the swagger stick began to assume the notorious, adorable features of her vanished sweetheart, Captain Eric. So Boadicea closed her eyes, and daydreamed. Then she opened her eyes, and decided.

There was only one thing to do. She must seize this opportunity to examine the layout of her sweetheart's ship, or rather his vehicle. It must surely hold the key to his plans and his hopes.

Boadicea rose to her paws, avid with eagerness. She set off along the warm channel of the gutter towards the fluted opening of the main drainpipe, wrapping an oak leaf round her shoulders to keep off the mud. The wind made a strange melancholy slithering noise in the dark pipe, very eerie, in fact, and not at all the sort of accompaniment for a calm May afternoon.

The journey downwards had all the ghostly sadness of November in it, and Boadicea shivered with more than the damp and cold as she came out through the overflow into the stone pit above the grate. It was a weird interlude in her dream, and her day. She pictured Eric as a mad laird in Scotland, with a chill castle on the brink of a sea loch and an icy, spiral stair down to the wave-lapped dungeon where his former wife was locked in a vault.

Breathless and cramped from her descent, Boadicea

paused by the grate to wipe her fur all over with the oak leaf. Then with a final shudder to cast off her wintry dream, she shinned up the stone wall of the overflow and jumped down into the sweet-smelling bed of lavender by the grey stucco of the wall.

Peering out, she could see the gleaming black of the car's mudguards only a few yards away. She was suddenly back in the glossy adventurous sparkle of the present.

7

The Embassy on Wheels

There was plenty of cover to hide Boadicea as she ran quickly along the wallflowers in front of the house and approached the motorcar from the side. As it happened, the presence of cover was fortunate, since there was one potential danger the little mouse had overlooked.

At the brink of the stone steps which led up to the massive painted oak panels of the front door, Boadicea paused. Sheltered by the overhang of the bull-nosing, she took a surreptitious glance at the moulded coachwork of the car. Her eye moved up over the grooved rubber running board, the glistening royal blue of the door panel, the curved brass of the loop handle, up to and, over and, yes, now in through the clear pane of the half-rolled-down window.

'Oh dear,' said Boadicea.

She shrank back under a wilting tea-rose to the left of the door.

'I must really be more careful,' she said to herself.

In the warm glow of her daydreaming and the excitement of seeing the young officer with the swagger stick, what Boadicea had entirely failed to check on was whether there was any other occupant of the motorcar. In fact, there was.

Exactly where he might have been expected, the stalwart bulk of a young man in the uniform of a private soldier was filling the hooped leather seat immediately behind the steering wheel. Boadicea had an uninterrupted view of him through the passenger's window.

As she watched, he was staring, apparently in a mood of stolid boredom, through the forward-looking glass of the windscreen. His right hand, in a motoring glove, was clenched on the stem of an empty pipe, which he appeared to be knocking up and down, in a more or less unconscious gesture, on some part of his body Boadicea couldn't see, but which she thought was probably his kneecap. Boadicea knew from observation of the rector's brother, who was a keen smoker, and frequently sat about in the library with a pipe and a book, that the knee was the usual place for a pipe to be knocked on.

Then, very obligingly from Boadicea's point of view, the soldier opened the car door and stepped down onto the drive. There he stood, slapping the pipe on the palm of his ungloved hand, and glaring moodily out at the rather exquisite blossoms of the wayfaring-tree.

Boadicea, like her brother Tamburlaine, was a bold young mouse and she seized her opportunity. Scuttling out from under the step, she was across the gravel, under the enormous oil-smelling factory of the motorcar's propelling mechanism, and out and up, with a quick spring, onto the top edge of the running board.

The soldier, who was still balefully assessing the shrubbery, had left the door swung open and it was easy

enough for Boadicea to climb over the sill and onto the carpeted floor of the interior. From there, sweltering in the baking heat from the uncooled engine, she glanced out at the soldier's firm back and his rather large, carroty ears.

Even as she watched, he half turned and began to walk away along the terrace, evidently eager to alleviate his boredom by some distraction. Boadicea turned her attention to the car.

The war had now been in progress, she knew from what Grandfather Mouse had told them, for several months, but this was the first time that she or any of the other mice had seen signs of a military presence within the confines of Oby rectory.

Boadicea, with her daydreaming and her eloquent fantasies of life with Eric, had clearly stumbled on something of importance. Guessing this, and allowing her daydream to expand again in the boiling summer-house of the car's upholstery, Boadicea commenced on a tour of inspection and inquiry.

First of all she leapt up onto the driver's seat. Above her the arched circuit of the steering wheel thrust forward beyond a fine array of dials and pointers. None of these meant very much to Boadicea, with the exception of a flat one containing the letters NSW and E. This was very like another one that she'd seen the rector's son holding once in the playroom, and she'd heard him speak its name.

'Compass,' she said to herself. 'They certainly won't get lost on their way home, wherever that is.'

The leather of the seat was extremely hot, and Boadicea found herself jumping up and down to prevent the soles of her paws from getting burned. She looked across at the passenger seat, anxious to find something a little cooler to sit on.

In her mind the car had by now become the embassy of a foreign power. The ingenious and beautiful spy Boadicea had broken in by night to discover the secret files which would enable her to locate the place where her sweetheart, the prominent arms manufacturer, Lord Eric, was being held to ransom.

'That's it,' said Boadicea to herself.

On the opposite seat, her eye had fallen on something that seemed likely to satisfy both of her requirements, the need for a cooler place to stand and some explanation of why the motorcar had come to the house. It might even, who knows, enable her to free her incarcerated Lord Eric from his captors.

Boadicea made skilful use both of her paws and her tail and, in only a few seconds, she was across the gap between the driving and the passenger seats and safely standing on a long sheet of foolscap neatly attached by a couple of drawing pins to a rather hard-looking and somewhat military board.

Beyond the car, she could hear the crunch of the soldier's footsteps, as he walked to and fro on the terrace, waiting. From time to time, she caught a glimpse of his waist, as he momentarily blocked her view of the flowering currant on his way past the open door.

Boadicea stood up again on her hind paws, and looked down at the long sheet of paper. She could see that it was largely covered in a black, rather sprawling handwriting and she walked up to the top of the page so that she could try to read it over in order.

The paper had a specially printed heading, which felt ridged and rounded, like a kind of braille, to Boadicea's paw. She spelled the words out to herself.

1st Battalion, Norfolk Light Infantry, she read.

It sounded very grand, and rather threatening too, she thought. It would obviously prove invaluable in her search for the carefully hidden away and adorable Lord Eric. So she read on, tracing the first words of the handwritten message with her paw.

Instructions for the. Boadicea put her head on one side. The next word was a difficult one and she couldn't quite make out the first letters. The word seemed to be something like millet or pellets but it was longer than both of those.

Boadicea took a sensible decision. She went back over the words she knew, jumped the one she didn't and read on to try and get the meaning from what came next. Unfortunately, it didn't really help. *Instructions for the* something like millet or pellets *of C Company* was what the sentence said.

Boadicea shook her head. She'd better read a few

sentences more, she thought. Arranging herself more comfortably, she lay down so that she could trace the lines with her paw while she rested on her side.

At this very moment, however, there was a loud interruption, and one that sent Boadicea scampering off the seat and down out of sight under the overhang of the dashboard before you could say even quite a short word like whippersnapper.

'Swish old motor,' a voice drawled, almost, it seemed, directly above poor Boadicea's astonished head.

It wasn't, however, where the voice came from that worried Boadicea. She'd heard human voices often enough before above her head. It was whose this voice was that sent her scuttling so fast for cover.

The mice had all found by bitter experience that the sound of this voice almost invariably preceded trouble. Trouble with a capital T. Trouble in the shape of nastily spinning wooden tops that curled round and followed you into corners. Trouble in the shape of deliberately aimed stones from enormous catapults. Worst of all, Trouble in the shape of their enemy, the cats, dragging like a willing and hungry bodyguard at the voice's heels.

Boadicea cowered down. She didn't try to look out. She knew exactly what she would see. The rector's seven-year-old son, yawning and vicious in his immaculate sailor-suit. A rubber ball or a tin whistle in his whitened, cruel hands.

Oh yes, Boadicea knew precisely what she would see.

'Very swish,' the voice repeated.

8
Human Voices

There was a crunch of boots on gravel, and then the sound of a hand slapping metal.

'Napier town carriage,' said a rough, masculine voice. 'With a Mulliner body. She's a real booty.'

'Beeooty,' Boadicea heard the rector's boy say and then add, in his horrid lisping drawl for that's how it always sounded to the mice, 'You ought to learn to pronounce words properly.'

The soldier laughed. He had a loud, rasping laugh and he didn't sound at all put out by the boy's rudeness.

'That's how we talk in Norfolk,' he said. 'You'll know that well enough when you're older. Father just come out here from somewhere farther off, possibly?'

The last sentence he made a question, but not one he appeared very interested in hearing the answer to.

'I've been here all my life,' the boy snorted. 'And I know perfectly well how people in Norfolk talk. They should still learn how to pronounce beeooty properly. It's a word one uses a lot, you know.'

The soldier laughed again.

'So what's your name?' he asked. 'You sound a proper old clever Dick to me.'

'My name's Montgomery,' the boy said. 'And I'll thank you not to be insolent. My father's the rector here, you know. And my uncle,' he added, as if realizing that this further revelation might carry even greater weight, 'is a Colonel in the Shropshire Borderers. They're in France just now. Fighting the Germans.'

Boadicea uncurled herself and took a peek out of the open door. She couldn't see very much, though, from where she was crouched under the passenger seat. Only the back of the soldier's leg and the high shine of his boots.

'And what's *your* name?' the boy was continuing.

'Elvin,' the soldier said. 'Private Elvin of the Fourteenth regiment Norfolk Light Infantry. At your service, Mr Monty.'

'I'm glad to hear you're at my service,' the boy said. 'But please don't call me mister. My full name is Montgomery St John Sutcliffe. And, as you're a private soldier, you'd better call me sir.'

The soldier, who was evidently a very self-possessed young man, was clearly much amused by this snobbish instruction. Boadicea could hear him chuckling to himself.

'Well, thank you, *sir*,' he said, with a heavy emphasis on the last word, 'but I think I'll just stick with Monty. Tell me,' he went on quickly, before the boy could interrupt, 'would you like a ride round the grounds in the motorcar?'

At this, Boadicea was immediately tense again. She had two choices, either to stay still and risk being caught in the car, or to leap for freedom and risk being seen and

pursued into the shrubbery. She paused, deliberating. The driver's door was being opened wider, and the young soldier was beginning to describe the interior to a by now slightly mollified Montgomery St John Sutcliffe.

'The windows go up and down like a train's,' Elvin was saying. 'You see. You just pull this leather strap, and it notches down at one or other of these holes on a little brass stud in the door.'

Boadicea could see the tail of the strap for the front passenger's window dangling down only a few inches above her quivering whiskers. For a brief moment she felt it merging into the twisted rope of bedsheets down which the intrepid Lord Eric was shinning to Boadicea and safety from the lofty attic window of his prison. Then reality took over again and she made her decision.

The driver's doorway was now completely blocked by the khaki tunic of Private Elvin and the wide blue sailor's collar of young Monty. There was a rough, hairy fist on the rim of the glass screen which cut off the rear portion of the saloon. It would be impossible to get out through the driver's door without being seen, and probably caught, on the way.

On the other hand, the lieutenant would in due course return from the house and the passenger door would be held open for him. At that moment, when everyone was looking out or up, it should be fairly easy for an agile mouse to skip nimbly down into the wallflowers and make off round the side of the library.

So Boadicea waited.

'You see that little hole in the windscreen,' said Private Elvin, very officious and proud now that he was master of the grand tour. 'Well that's for the driver to see through when it rains and the rest of the glass gets misted up or covered in water. Very useful little aperture, that hole.'

'I dare say,' said the boy. 'But I'll bet it gets rather cold. I imagine it must send blasts of icy air right into your eye.'

At this moment, there was another sound, somewhere behind young Boadicea's back as she hunched up making herself as small as she could against the dirty carpeting. It was a distant mutter of voices, accompanied by footsteps. She watched the faces of the young soldier and the boy withdraw. Then she heard the front door opening and guessed that her moment to escape was at hand.

'So I'm glad, very glad, we can be of some assistance,' she heard a new voice pronounce, a very hearty and at the same time rather solemn and measured voice. Boadicea knew that voice very well.

She had heard it saying grace once over Sunday luncheon, as she scampered home from a walk in the skirting boards. She had heard it several times as it filtered up through the ceiling of the study, rehearsing the sonorous periods of a carefully meditated sermon.

It was a rich and practised voice, but one that was full of kindness too, and Boadicea was prepared to treat it with reverence. She pictured the rector, from whom this balanced music emanated, as he would be on the steps in his morning suit, with his remaining hair brushed up round his ears and his bushy sideboards making up for the shining absence of any tufts on his skull.

He was a tall man and he was bound to be towering over his visitor, no doubt with a benign smile on his crinkling face. Boadicea got ready. She knew that the rector was bound to attract all eyes. When the passenger door was opened she had to go. And go fast.

'The men will arrive next Tuesday, then,' said another voice, a lighter and crisper one, which Boadicea assumed must belong to the lieutenant.

'Whenever your people choose,' she heard the rector saying. 'I'll ask my agent to have the granary and the hayloft cleared. They'll be warm enough out there while the summer lasts. They can wash at the pump. And they'll eat in the kitchen here with the servants.'

'You've been awfully generous,' said the other voice. 'I wish it was always so easy to billet the troops. I'm sure that my Colonel will want to call and say his thank yous in person.'

'He'll be very welcome,' said the rector. 'Tell him he'll find a glass of Madeira whenever he cares to call by.'

The door was wide open now and Boadicea could see the figure of Private Elvin standing to attention beside it.

'I say, father,' she heard young Monty say in his most casual drawl. 'This fellow here has promised me a drive down to Norwich in the motor.'

Boadicea went through the door at this point like a streak of rain across a window. She didn't wait to hear what excuse or explanation for this bluntly misconstrued offer poor Elvin might have to falter into. She didn't wait to see if the car would begin to move with the monstrous Monty arranged in state on the smart young lieutenant's lap.

She dived for the bed of flowers, inviting, wonderful yellows along the flaking stucco. In her mind Lord Eric and she were racing for the cover of a Scottish grouse moor under a hail of Prussian machine-gun bullets. The British army and its billets – or pellets, or whatever they were – were not, for the moment, her worry.

9
The Soldiers Arrive

It was Uncle Trinity who saw the soldiers arrive. He was
up on the ridge pole of the dairy, taking a look from
below at the position of the box round the offensive bell
which disturbed the mice so much in the mornings.
Michaelmas had suggested that he cast his expert eye on
the problem.

Uncle Trinity was flattered to be asked, but the actual
investigation had proved something of a nuisance. He
was a rather fat, red-faced farmer of a mouse and his
bulk was better suited to carting wheat ears and berries
in from the fields than to clambering about like a young
squirrel on top of a roof.

Anyway, that's how he was putting it to himself this
warm June morning as he puffed and grunted his way
through the culminating scrolls of decorative ironwork.
He was feeling hot and bothered and he'd much rather
have been dipping into a slice or two of wild strawberry
than gallivanting here in a rusting wilderness of iron
fleur-de-lys.

The roof was due for a church inspection shortly and the paint of the rail had been allowed to flake and peel off. It made it easier for Uncle Trinity to get a grip and weave his way along, but it also left a good deal of rust in this dry weather, and it tended to kick up and make him sneeze.

'Play the devil with my sinus this will,' he muttered to himself, as he reached the angle where three roofs met, and was able to lean back in a bracket of curved iron and stare straight up into the cavity of the bell.

It didn't look at all satisfactory. The clapper was on the outside of the bell and there seemed no obvious way in which it could be padded. Perhaps, after all, the mice would either have to gnaw through the rope or simply forget about any action and make the best of it.

'Very nasty,' said Uncle Trinity later, when he reported on the situation to Michaelmas over a glass of cool snowberry ale.

At the time, however, he said nothing at all, but simply turned around on his ample bottom to enjoy the view out over the fields to Ashby Hall. And there, at first remote in the distance as a line of tiny brown figures at the crossroads, and then more near as a noise of steady, regular tramping, and then quite close as a winding shape of rods and khaki circles beyond the track to the village of Repps, and then finally, suddenly, almost underneath his alert nose as Uncle Trinity peered down from his flourishing belvedere, were the twenty or thirty marching British soldiers who were going, by the grace and favour of the rector, to be billeted in the granary and the hayloft.

Uncle Trinity was a patriotic mouse and he watched them with a sense of pride. If it hadn't been for his natural mouse caution he would have raised a solitary cheer or a 'bravo' or 'well done, lads'.

The soldiers were all in step, and they moved with a fine, rather dashing movement along the fluid white of the hawthorn. Each man had his cap set at the same, precise, military angle and his well-polished Lee Enfield rifle firmly grasped at the butt and laid along the bone of the shoulder.

They made a pretty sight in their light khaki, their brass and metal glinting in the sun and Uncle Trinity was reminded, as he watched, of some lines of poetry he'd heard the rector intoning aloud one evening after dinner when he was entertaining the family in the drawing room before bed. He remembered the slim vellum book and the rector's fine baritone as he said:

> And you will list the bugle
> That blows in lands of morn,
> And make the foes of England
> Be sorry you were born.

That put it rather well, Uncle Trinity thought, and he said the lines over to himself in his own more tenor tones as he watched the soldiers pass by the double gates, a bold square-shouldered sergeant with a huge Kitchener moustache striding along beside them, and then tramp away, tramp tramp, tramp tramp towards the muddy lane which wound to the farm.

'Le-ft, Wheel,' Uncle Trinity heard a rasping, porty voice announce, and then there was a change in the tramp tramp sound, and he knew that the soldiers were turning in towards the yard and the barns.

Uncle Trinity sucked in his breath.

'Exactly as young Boadicea predicted,' he said to himself. 'We're being billeted with a company of infantrymen.'

And he bustled down off the roof to tell the other mice the news. Excited as they all were to know about

these new arrivals, it was a day or two before more information of their doings began to filter through.

Amelia Mouse came home one day with a story of how the men were settled comfortably in the granary, with their wooden camp beds all folded forward, and their plain deal stools laid out with brushes and polish for keeping their equipment clean. She saw all this at close quarters when she smuggled a lift for herself round to the farm kitchen in the cart that went for eggs and potatoes, and she told the other mice they could rest assured that the soldiers were safe and sound and well installed.

There were soon other scraps of information too, one from Michaelmas about a couple of soldiers playing scratch cricket together outside the pig-sty, with a stick of firewood and a tennis ball, and then one from Boadicea about the sergeant picking out mournful tunes on a battered mouth organ by the light of a candle. But these were civilian pastimes, the mice longed to know more of how the soldiers were preparing to go to war.

It was Tamburlaine who found out. He didn't like being indoors during the summer weather and he spent a lot of time exercising his muscles in the wood and the hedgerows. He was inclined, in fact, or so one might say, to go out looking for trouble.

One afternoon about a week after the soldiers' arrival, Taburlaine had gone wandering through the cotoneaster hedge which stood on the brink of the old ha-ha at the boundary of the rectory lawn and the three-acre field. The ha-ha had been dug many years before to keep out the pasturing livestock, but in recent times, when the field had been used more for horses than cattle, the ditch had been supplemented with a hedge.

This hedge was a frequent haunt of field mice, and the young Tamburlaine was very fond of challenging one of these to a mock fight or a race through the underbrush. There was the hollowed stump of a dead elm at one end of the hedge and the outer rim of this, with its crenellated edge, made an excellent point of vantage.

Tamburlaine, like a border baron in his castle, would lie in wait here and plunge forth to harry the innocent passersby. Mercifully, he'd so far had the good sense to confine his attentions to mice of his own size.

This morning very few other mice seemed to be about, and Tamburlaine had taken to staring rather dreamily out across the field, of which he had a splendid view from where he crouched. At a distance of about a hundred yards there was a line of fine sycamores, acting as a wind-break against the vicious winds from the marsh lands near the River Bure. In front of these an earlier rector, with a taste for the sports of more stirring days, had erected a row of butts, and the cork rings of the targets formed a reminder of the great battles of Agincourt and Crécy.

As Tamburlaine was eyeing these and vaguely wondering how his sister Boadicea would have imagined the noble rats who might have drawn their bows in days of yore, a line of khaki figures emerged from the oak wood at the end of the rectory garden. Several of these figures were jointly supporting awkward-shaped lumps of canvas in their arms and most of the rest were laden with the usual paraphernalia of soldiers on the march, rifles, bandoliers, water bags and bayonets.

Tamburlaine woke up and began to pay attention. At last the soldiers were going to do something interesting! As he watched, adjusting his tail round himself for more comfort, the men began to erect a series of wooden racks, or miniature gallows, from each of which they hung by ropes a roughly-moulded sack-like object in the shape of a human torso.

The sergeant went to and fro, tapping these hanging objects with a stick and generally making small alterations to the way they were arranged. When he seemed satisfied, he stood back and began to give loud, parade-ground orders.

The soldiers all leapt to attention and began to raise and lower their rifles, stand at ease and to attention and march up and down as the sergeant instructed them. All this was taking place against the background of the silent, all-seeing eyes of the archery targets.

At last, the sergeant seemed satisfied with the preliminary drill. He walked up and down the standing row of men, talking in a more quiet voice that Tamburlaine couldn't quite make out. Occasionally, he would point at the row of hanging objects and make a sudden jerking, thrusting movement with his hands. Then, stepping away, he gave a final order in loud, ringing tones that carried clearly across the field to where Tamburlaine was crouched.

'Fix bayonets!'

This order was given with a loving dwelling on the f and the b, as if the sergeant thought the beginning of his words required extra special emphasis. But at this very interesting, and unusual moment, young Tamburlaine's attention was distracted.

He heard a faint rustle in the twigs below the hedge. Someone was coming. Peering down, he could see the sleek figure of a mouse, partly obscured by the fans of tiny green leaves, approaching the ruined stump from the direction of the house.

Inflamed by the heady rhetoric of war from the field, and eager for some more immediate excitement than the onlooker's one of watching the soldiers at exercise, Tamburlaine climbed up onto the ridge of his castle and prepared to leap. The strange mouse, who seemed to be coming towards him all unawares, was only a foot or two away.

Now, Taburlaine thought, and plunged.

10
Some Thoughts on War

Even as he fell, Tamburlaine realized that he'd made a mistake. The newcomer pushing through the leaves was a good deal bigger than he'd seemed at first and, worse than that, or perhaps after all, rather better than that, he also looked horribly familiar.

'Got you,' said Tamburlaine anyway, deciding in the split second that he landed on the bigger mouse's back that he'd be best advised to make this unseemly assault appear as a jolly game.

He felt his forepaws clutching at a well-known muscular back, his nose rubbing on a powerful neck, and then, splumph, he was flying up in the air again, the sky and the field and the leaves all turning a ludicrous somersault round his ears, and then, blumph, kerwallop, splat, he had landed flat on his back, all the breath knocked out of his body, and a fierce, irritated set of ginger whiskers was bristling down at him.

In the distance, Tamburlaine heard the sound of running footsteps, followed by a long-drawn-out aaaaaaaaaaaaaargh sound, and then something like a sack tearing open. He blinked, gasping for breath, and stared up in horror directly into his father's by no means delighted or forgiving eyes.

'Hmmn,' said Michaelmas to begin with, dusting his paws.

Then he helped Tamburlaine up and brushed bits of twig and leaf off him.

'I'm sorry, father,' said Tamburlaine, hopefully. 'I really am.'

Michaelmas frowned.

'Let's go into the stump,' he said. 'It's safer there.'

So the two mice, father and son, climbed up the ruined side of the stump and into what had so recently been Tamburlaine's frontier castle. It seemed now, to the sorrowful and guilty little Tamburlaine, more like a punishment room, or a medieval dungeon.

'I was only playing, father,' he faltered out. 'You see, I thought you were a field mouse or a small vole.'

Michaelmas was gazing down across the field, where the line of soldiers were again back in position, aligning their fixed bayonets for a second charge. The sergeant was fingering his large moustache.

'I'm a good deal bigger than a vole,' said Michaelmas in some annoyance. 'And that's exactly the point, my boy. If you can't tell the difference in size between an adult mouse and a half-grown vole then you haven't any business playing dangerous games of hide-and-seek. Or hunt your neighbour,' he corrected himself.

'I'm sorry,' said Tamburlaine.

The soldiers had begun to run. They moved slowly

over the rough, pot-holed ground, and one tripped and stumbled before recovering his balance and running on. The sergeant watched, one hand on his hip.

'Aaaaaaaaaaaaargh,' the soldiers shouted.

Then, one by one, they began to thrust forward and ram their bayonets through the hanging canvas objects, then withdraw, stand back and ram them in again.

'Aaaaaaaaaargh,' they would each shout, with varying degrees of savagery, as they did this.

'Why do they all shout like that, father?' asked Tamburlaine as he stared down over Michaelmas's shoulder.

'Don't change the subject,' said Michaelmas. 'You've behaved in a very silly and potentially dangerous way.

If it hadn't been me you landed on, you might have been badly knocked about or even killed. You'll be banned from going outdoors on your own for two full days. For the moment, I'll say no more about it.'

Tamburlaine breathed a sigh of relief. He knew that his father could be very severe over breaches of discipline which in his view involved some risk of life or limb, and the punishment now imposed was considerably less than he'd expected. He'd feared that he might be kept indoors for a week.

'You see,' said Michaelmas, in a less reprimanding, but equally serious tone of voice, 'it's a good deal easier to kill someone if you make a loud noise about it. That's why the sergeant makes the soldiers all shout aloud when they drive their bayonets in.'

Tamburlaine listened carefully as he watched a particularly tall, heavily-built soldier, who was bellowing out a whole string of angry-sounding words and forcing his bayonet into the hanging sack again and again. The sergeant walked over and put a hand on his shoulder.

'Well done, lad,' Tamburlaine heard him say. 'That's enough for now.'

Tamburlaine leaned back on a pile of crumbled wood and looked away for a moment over towards the south façade of the rectory. The afternoon sun was glancing along the drawing room window, which was half-open, and the rector's younger daughter was playing with a doll in a trundle-cart on the gravel terrace between the urns. It was a peaceful scene.

'Tell me something, father,' said Tamburlaine. 'I can understand why people want to keep their houses for themselves, and why they sometimes put out traps for us and set the cats on us to kill us. But why do they want to kill each other? Isn't that very wasteful?'

Michaelmas rumpled his son's ear. It wasn't often that they had a chance to talk alone together, and he quite welcomed the opportunity to say something serious.

'It's the way people are,' he said sadly. 'They seem to enjoy making war, I don't know why. If we mice did the same, there would very soon be none of us left.'

The soldiers had broken ranks and were squatting in a rough circle, paying attention to a lengthy lecture on tactics the sergeant was delivering. His voice, quieter now, carried over the summer field as a low murmur. It mingled with the hum of bees and the gentle soughing of the wind.

'Our lives are more extreme,' said Michaelmas, when he and his son had been silent for a while. 'We mice are at war, in a way, against our environment. We have to be constantly on watch to survive.'

'You mean we don't have time to kill each other,' said Tamburlaine with his tongue in his cheek.

His father cuffed him affectionately.

'You know I don't,' he said. 'I wouldn't want to kill your Uncle Trinity if he was the last mouse in the world. We're part of the same family. With people,' he added sadly, 'that doesn't seem to have sunk in yet. They're not as evolved, you see, as we are, as a species.'

Round the side of the house, from the dairy, the odd-job boy appeared, awkwardly walking with a deep basket chair held in each hand. Behind him came the chambermaid, spick and span in her black dress and apron, with a folding table under her arm.

'Frittering their time away with afternoon tea and scones,' said Michaelmas testily. 'You'd think they'd got nothing better to do. We mice gave up all that sort of thing centuries ago.'

Tamburlaine watched the boy arranging the chairs on

the lawn between the windows. He was a clumsy, shock-headed young fellow, with baggy trousers and a thick belt. The maid, with her red hair and her freckles, upbraided his awkwardness. She was quick and bright, like a prize hen at the hocks of a calf.

'You mind them chairs now, Norman,' Tamburlaine heard her say and he watched the boy skulk off round the house, frowning. The maid remained, fussing with a lace tablecloth and a handful of linen napkins.

'Have you ever been at war, father?' said Tamburlaine. 'I mean with other animals.'

'It was very like a war,' said Michaelmas. 'Very like a war, when we lost our homes in the harvest-field. You don't remember, of course. You weren't born then.'

Tamburlaine sat up very straight, and was instantly all ears.

'Tell me about it, father,' he said.

So Michaelmas curled up his tail round his lean flanks and leaned back against the rotten wall of the stump and, while the afternoon sun burned the resting soldiers in the meadow and warmed the servants for whom they were fighting as they laid tea on the rectory lawn, he told his son for the first time the grim and violent story of how he and his brother Trinity had been forced to leave their lofty houses amidst the wheat-ears and seek refuge indoors at the rectory high up in the draughty and languorous rafters.

It was a long story, and it held Tamburlaine entranced until suppertime, when the shadows began to lengthen and the dangerous twilight of the owl-time approached. But Michaelmas was far too cautious a father to take any further risks that day and he made sure his narrative drew to an end and his son was taken indoors well before the first bat spread its wings from the barn, and swooped in front of the acacia.

He curtailed his narrative and held back some of the more atrocious parts as being too horrifying for a little mouse to hear, but he told his story well.

11
Afternoon Tea on the Lawn

'You see,' said Michaelmas as he lay back with his paws crossed in the safety of the stump, 'at one time we used to live out of doors all spring and summer and only come in to the rafters for the winter. We built our grass houses in one of the rector's fields, whichever one was planted with corn that year, and nobody disturbed us until the harvest.

'The field we chose would vary,' said Michaelmas. 'Sometimes we'd be over towards the Fleggburgh side and sometimes nearer the village of Thurne. It all depended on the rotation of crops and the chances of finding a nice, isolated spot in the wheat or barley.'

'Tell me about the rotation of crops,' said Tamburlaine as he watched the strawberries.

'Every year,' said his father, 'they plant a different crop in each field. One year it's oats, perhaps, and another potatoes. And then they allow the field to rest for a year. That's called letting it lie fallow. Whenever a field was empty, of course, we couldn't use it. We'd have been exposed to the hunting owls in no time.'

'But couldn't you have built your houses in the wild grass?' asked Tamburlaine. 'It would surely have grown up rather high when the field wasn't planted with corn.'

Michaelmas patted his son on the nose.

'Good for you,' he said. 'You're using your brain. Well, we could, of course. But the farmers used the empty fields for their sheep, and sometimes horses, to graze in. And very soon they were eaten down as bald as a bowling green. So we used to go from field to field, wherever there was somewhere to build and something to eat.

'The fields we chose would vary and so, of course, would the times of harvest. We knew from experience that it all depended on the kind of weather we were having. The farmers liked to wait until the ears of corn were brown, on the whole, but they didn't like to be caught by a spell of heavy rain and have to leave their stooks out of doors too long to dry before the threshing.'

'What's threshing?' asked Tamburlaine.

He brushed his back gently where a little fly had settled. The mice were always careful with the flying and walking insects they encountered. They had no taste for meat and so no temptation to hunt or kill them for food. And the various caterpillars and spiders and kinds of bees and bluebottles they met with had no inclination to do them any harm. So there was a mutual pact of courtesy.

'Threshing,' said Michaelmas as he watched the fly disappear in a glossy pagoda of holly leaves, 'is the way men separate the grain from the chaff. In the olden

days, they did it with long wooden brushes called flails
in a kind of barn, but nowadays they have special new
machines, with steam engines. And a fearsome noise
they make about it, too,' he added grimly.

'The time of harvest varies,' resumed Michaelmas,
after a pause during which he had taken in the
continuing preparations for tea on the terrace. 'But we
used to be able to predict when the day might come. We
mice are all pretty accurate forecasters of weather, you
know.'

'Not always,' objected Tamburlaine. He remembered
several occasions when Grandfather Mouse had tapped
his pine cone and insisted that the weather was set fair
and when he, Tamburlaine, accepting this pronounce-
ment as like the laws of God, had in consequence gone
for a long walk without a laurel leaf umbrella and thus
got thoroughly soaked.

'Not always,' he insisted.

It was a characteristic of Tamburlaine that he liked to
have the last word and his proneness to contradict his
elders had often got him into trouble. But by now his
father was absorbed in his narrative and inclined to be
lenient to contradiction.

'Normally,' he said firmly, 'we mice are extremely
good prophets of rain. But not always,' he conceded.
'And that's exactly the point, in my story. It's precisely
because we were always so good at knowing when the
weather would change from fine to stormy that we came
to rely so absolutely on our natural gifts. We didn't
bother to watch out for signs of an early harvest
independent of the state of the weather.'

Michaelmas stretched his legs. He was feeling a little
stiff, perhaps with the awful tension of remembering.

'One year,' he said simply, 'we were taken unawares.

And that's when we decided to alter our life style and live indoors all the year round.'

'That was a big decision,' said Tamburlaine, wrenching his attention away from the lawn. 'I mean, to come and live indoors for always, just because you once got caught out about the time of the harvest.'

'Yes,' agreed Michaelmas. 'It was a very big decision. But it was absolutely the right one. You see, the consequences of our failure to predict the time of the harvest were rather catastrophic.'

'What's catastrophic?' asked Tamburlaine.

'Things going wrong,' said Michaelmas. 'Very wrong. That's what catastrophic is. Being made homeless. Near starvation. Sudden death of your dear ones. That's what war can be. And that's what the night harvest was for us.'

'Catastrophic,' said Tamburlaine slowly so as to get

the sound right in his mind. 'It sounds terrible. Sort of like "strife" and "awful". It has a cat in it, too.'

'Words with cat in,' said Michaelmas generalizing with a broad unfairness, 'are usually pretty bad ones. You can be sure of that.' And then, since he could only for the moment think of catamite and catafalque and he didn't feel that either of these were quite within Tamburlaine's compass, he hurried on with his story. 'So make yourself comfortable, my boy,' he said, 'and I'll tell you exactly what happened.'

12
The Night Harvest

'We had a lovely ball house,' said Michaelmas, 'at the top of a stalk of barley. It was woven out of grasses and barley leaves, and your mother and I were especially proud of it. There was plenty of space for both of us and also for your elder brothers, Horatius and Caesar Mouse.'

'What happened to them?' asked Tamburlaine, luxuriating in the hot sun through the holly leaves.

Michaelmas ignored the question. He meant to tell the story in his own way and in his own time. And the fate of his two sons from those days was not the aspect he most wanted to dwell on or, at any rate, not at the beginning of his narrative.

'We had a granary for our corn,' he said, 'and a rose hip store for autumn berries and your Uncle Trinity and his family had a place of their own only a few stalks away. We were almost a little village, high above the ground, out there under the great oak tree you can see behind the butts.'

'In the rectory meadow,' said Tamburlaine.

'In the rectory meadow,' his father confirmed. 'The year I'm talking about we had old King Edward still on the throne, God bless his soul, and the finest spread of barley there they'd known since the Afghan Wars. It was waving gold in the wind from here to the sycamores and the road to Manor Farm.'

'Were there lots of mice in the field?' asked Tamburlaine.

'There were many mice,' his father said, 'and there were quite a few we knew and some we visited. Only your Uncle Trinity and his family, though, were really close. The others were mostly down by the corner of the wood, where you see the hawthorn.'

Michaelmas paused, stroking his fur down with his paws with a mannerism he often had when he was preoccupied.

'When the crisis came that night,' he said slowly, 'most of the mice went over towards the Glebe Farm, through the trees. There was more cover there, to escape by. And more new homes to find in the barns. Quite a few are there still. You've met your cousin Ethelred when he's travelled over in the milk cart.'

'Yes, and Minx and Dotty, too,' said Tamburlaine, remembering his white, fussy cousins, with their black ruffs, blue eyes and high giggling laughs. Privately, he thought they were very silly, but he was too prudent to say so to his father, who was a great stickler for speaking well of one's relations.

'They're good souls, Ethelred and his family,' said Michaelmas, illustrating this principle on cue. 'I'm glad they were able to make their way through the wood.'

'Tell me what happened, father,' said Tamburlaine. 'Tell me exactly, please. Don't jump about so much and leave things out. It makes it hard to follow.'

Michaelmas reached out and patted his son's ear.

'I'm sorry,' he said. 'I keep forgetting you weren't there and I get distracted. I'll come directly to the point.

'I woke up,' he said, 'well after dark and well before dawn. It was completely black so far as I could see. Your mother and the two children were fast asleep. At first, I thought that I'd been having a bad dream. I felt very strange, though without exactly being able to say why. There was something wrong, and I couldn't think what it was. Then I felt it again, the thing that had wakened me. A sort of steady, deep rumbling in the ground. Like wheels. Like the sound of horses' hoofs. Like a great number of men walking.

'I knew in a flash what it was. I'd heard it so many times before, year after year. In the mornings, in the afternoons. With the sun rising in the eastern horizon, or sinking towards the west. At many different times. But never, never, never like now in the dead middle of the night, without warning, in absolute darkness.

'I knew that it couldn't be the same thing. It had to be something else. My dream, perhaps. I pinched myself. No, I was wide awake, just as I knew I was. I could feel the warm dry grass brushing my face, hear the faint rustle of the stalks all round, see now the vague sleeping shapes of Amelia and your two brothers beside me.

'See? Why, it must be the dawn coming. They must be starting early. But no, it couldn't be dawn. I'd have been awake already, I always slept where the first early beam could run in and catch my eye the moment it crept above the horizon. This wasn't the sun. It was getting lighter all the time, though, and the noise was louder, the usual noise, the heavy fearsome inevitable rumble and beat I knew so very well.

'They were starting the harvest. It had never happened before this way, in the middle of the night, with men carrying hurricane lamps to light the way for the reapers. It was something I'd never heard of, never experienced. Normally, the harvest would start very early one morning, and the previous day we'd have seen the horse-drawn waggons arrive with the extra hands hired from far and wide to cut and stack the corn. Occasionally, when there was a threat of rain, they'd make a start after lunch and begin reaping the day they arrived.

'But this was something unique. I know now from stories and books I've seen that a harvest can happen any time, and a wise mouse is one who is ready at all times. That year the farmer had a premonition that we were in for a summer thunderstorm, and he wanted to have his barley stooked in the field as soon as he could. He must have lain awake in the darkness and then made a sudden decision. He'd start at once.

'I can imagine the women there in the kitchen, tipping the great cans of paraffin and filling the metal reservoirs of the lamps to the brim. Drops falling sometimes to the flagged floor in their haste. Wicks being trimmed. Even candles pressed into sockets in old lanterns.

'And then the rush to wake the men and help them dress. Leather gaiters being fitted, scarves round necks for the chill. The whole rapid sleepy process of getting ready unexpectedly for a great endeavour in the middle of the night.

'For me it was different. I had no time to work all this out then and there, with the tramp of feet already in the field. I had to wake Amelia and your brothers, and get them started wrapping up the few vital things we needed to take along. A few leaves. A jar or two of preserves. Heirlooms. Toys.

'Trinity, luckily, was also awake, and I met him at the

bottom of the stalk, still rubbing sleep out of his puffy eyes and shivering a little in the cold air.

' "Trinity," I said. "We have to move fast. I recommend we go for the rectory. It's near, and the men will be working in from the road and the wood."

'I remember your Uncle trying to think. He was just as tired-looking as I felt myself.

' "It's a risk," he said. "We'll have to cross the lawn in full view of any hunting owls and then we'll need to find some way to get in. We could use the stables, of course."

' "I don't think so," I said. "Every mouse in the field is going to rush for the farm, and the ones who're lucky are going to need a lot of space. Quite a few will have to come over the wall to the stables and the carriage house. We'll be better off in the rectory cellars. Not many others will go for there. Besides, we'll have no chance if we try to break through the line of the reapers. We'll be cut to bits."

' "All right," said your Uncle Trinity. "Let's try for the house."

'By now your mother and the children had come down the stalk, each clutching a little pack of essentials for the journey. Trinity's wife and his daughter, Gioconda, were approaching over the dew-wet soil. Everything seemed to be heaving and rumbling now, and we almost felt we could hear the slash and hiss of the blades against the necks of the barley.

'Above us towered the lovely, bending grasses we'd lived in all year and were having to leave in such dire haste. Ahead of us, away from the sloping beams of the hurricane lamps and the tread of the reapers, there was a ditch, the slope, this cotoneaster hedge, and then the lawn and the rectory.

'I made sure we were all together and then we set off as fast as we could.'

Throughout this narrative Tamburlaine had crouched spell-bound in the stump, entirely neglectful both of tea on the lawn and target practice in the field. As Michaelmas paused to collect his thoughts, Tamburlaine clapped his paws together in excitement and with approval.

'Don't stop,' he said. 'It's wonderful.'

13
A Tale of Bravery

'Wonderful,' said Michaelmas. 'It certainly wasn't that. Violence and sudden death are never wonderful. Terrible, yes. Exciting, maybe. But never wonderful.'

'I didn't exactly know there was violence and sudden death,' said Tamburlaine apologetically. 'I mean,' he added, 'I knew that there was, or was going to be. But you've mostly stressed the general side so far. The waking up in the night and the running away through the corn. It all sounds really quite good fun so far.'

'I suppose it does,' agreed Michaelmas. 'And perhaps it was, too, to begin with. Extreme situations are often rather enjoyable in their early stages. That's the trouble. You start to be almost proud of your power to cope with them, and then the crisis comes. And, splat, you're out of your depth.'

'Tell me about it, father,' said Tamburlaine quietly. 'Tell me the truth. The whole truth.'

But Michaelmas was hardly ready to go so far. The

memory of that awful night was clarifying in his mind
and the emotions it brought back with it were almost too
powerful for him to control. He waded on, up to his
knees in the story, but advancing with care.

'We reached the edge of the field very fast,' he said.
'There were long beams of light straggling through the
lines of stalks and we could hear the whirr and slice of
the knives now, and occasionally a low word or two
from the reapers. Mostly, though, they were working in
silence, conserving their energy and not talking much.

'As far as I could tell, the men cutting from our left,
from the wood, were the nearest now, but I was pretty
sure we could reach the ha-ha and get down and up the
other side before they arrived.'

'What's a ha-ha?' asked Tamburlaine.

'It's a kind of ditch,' said Michaelmas. 'Men dig them
to mark a boundary and to stop their cattle crossing
from a field into a garden. It's call a ha-ha because
anyone walking was supposed to arrive at one with a
sense of surprise and say Ha! And then, Ha! again.'

'Hmnn,' said Tamburlaine, half not believing. 'It
doesn't sound a very likely explanation to me. At any
rate,' he hurried on, suddenly realizing that this
contradiction might strike his father as rude, 'I don't
imagine that you and mother and Horatius and Caesar
were taken by surprise that night by the ha-ha. You had
worse things to surprise you.'

'We did, indeed,' said Michaelmas. 'And, besides, we
knew the ditch was there. I'd shown it to the children
from the edge of the corn, and we'd looked down into it
from under the waving ears. It was always dangerous at
twilight there, because you had no cover. So I never let
the boys go down.

'That night was different though. We had no choice.

We had either to stay where we were and risk being
sliced apart by the sickles, or step down out of the barley
and run across the open ground to the shelter of the
hedge. Unfortunately, it wasn't just open ground either.
There was an easy slope down but then a very muddy
flat stretch, with some pools of water, and finally a
tormenting climb up the other side through tangled
roots and loose stones. And all the time we'd be out in
the air, albeit under cover of partial darkness, in the eye
of the owls.

'Well, there we all were at the edge of the field when,
suddenly, two things happened at once. First of all,
there was a tremendous crash and shattering noise and
a long flood of light and there, only a few feet away,
there was a huge, gaitered figure, one hand gripping the
stalks below the ears, another lifting a glittering moon-
shaped blade to sever the grain. Behind the man,
another was walking with a lifted hurricane lamp, the
double wick shedding a lurid glare over his unshaven
face, blunt nose, wide-set eyes.

'That was one thing. We had only a few seconds to
move before the very stalks we were standing under
would be seized and cut.

' "Move," I said. "Fast. All of you. Down the bank,
across, and up the other side. And don't stop or look
back for anything."

'I led the way. Head down, feet gripping, I started to
slither and tumble down the slope. Behind me I was
aware of the others following. And at that very moment
the second thing happened. It started to rain. There was
a tremendous thunderclap, right overhead it seemed,
and then the first few drops were a raging headlong
torrent.

'In a second I was drenched through. Out of the

corner of my eye I saw the light sliced into zig-zags by
the deluge, and I heard the men curse and swear and
then one saying, "Lookee there, George. The field do be
emptying out 'er mice tonight."

' "Rot t'mice, John," I heard another say. "This rain
do be goin' to ruin t'harvest if we not quick."

'Even as I swerved round a stone and squelched into
the muddy basin of the ditch, I remember registering
that they weren't local men. They sounded like hired
men over from another county. Dorset maybe, they
often came from there.

'Then I was reaching for a hold on a root, swinging
up, waiting, gathering breath, climbing on. I took a
moment to stop, looking over my shoulder. I know I'd
told the others not to stop, but I had to see where they
were. Amelia was close behind, Caesar out ahead
somewhere.

' "Horatius," I shouted to Amelia as she came level.
"Where's Horatius?"

'Amelia's face was streaming with rain. I don't think
she could hear me above the storm, but she too looked
back over her shoulder.

'There he was, halfway across the ditch. He was a little
mouse, not very fast on his feet. Even as I watched, there
was another thunderclap, and the rain came down in a
solid racing sheet. Through it, I saw the pools in the
ditch run and merge, Horatius fighting to free his feet
from the mud, then a sudden flood of water rush and
catch him in the chest.

'It all happened very quickly. One moment he was
there, struggling, swimming. The next he was gone, lost
somewhere out of sight. Then the rain was battering at
my grip, Amelia was fighting to hold on to an
embedded stone, there was nothing to do but climb.'

Michaelmas paused. There was a prolonged silence in the elm stump. Then Tamburlaine eased his cramped paws and said tentatively. 'You know, perhaps Horatius was washed up further down, and found his way to the barns. We may still meet him there, one day.'

'We may,' said his father sadly. 'But I'm afraid we won't ever see Caesar again. You see,' he said, shifting his position, 'Caesar was the sort of mouse you don't encounter very often. He was a bit lazy, and rather bad-tempered, in normal times. He wasn't really very clever either.'

Michaelmas paused, thinking.

'But he was very brave,' he said simply. 'It isn't always useful to be unusually brave. Sometimes, when times are easy, it just leads to trouble. Taking unnecessary risks and so on. It's when times are hard that we need the few who are really brave. Caesar was one of those.'

'Did you always know he was?' asked Tamburlaine.

'No,' said his father, 'I didn't. It was what he did when we crossed the lawn that showed me. You see, we were pretty tired, your mother and I, when we finally clambered up the slope and got under the shade of the cotoneaster hedge. We were soaked through too, and icily cold.

'There were still twenty yards or so of open grass, and then another yard of terrace, before we could reach the grating with a hole behind it through which we could squeeze into the cellar. After that, I knew the way we still use to get up to the attics and I was fairly confident I could avoid the barn owl on the way up.

'The crucial part was the journey across the lawn. It was totally open, without even a dandelion for cover. But we had to go straight over or make an exhausting detour through the shrubbery that I didn't think we'd ever survive.

'It was still raining, but a little less heavily. Caesar was to my right, Amelia crouched at my left shoulder.

' "Let's go," I said.

'I was halfway across, Amelia beside me, when I knew we were finished.'

Again, Michaelmas paused.

'It isn't a noise,' he continued, 'or anything you see, really. It's just that sense of the blanket of death settling over you from above. That's what it's like when you feel an owl diving. And I felt it then.

' "Freeze, freeze," I whispered.

'Then I was shivering, dead still, waiting, Amelia hard by me. And Caesar, too.'

Michaelmas took a breath.

'And then,' he said, with a throb in his voice, 'Caesar did what he did. Very deliberately, he knelt up on his back paws and twitched his whiskers. Then he started to trot casually forward under the levelling wings. I saw the huge grey piece of the sky break off and collapse onto his back, the hooked talons reaching, the beak open-red like a furnace.

'Then we were both running. Scuttling as fast as we could for the grating. Squeezing through. Panting. Safe indoors. Wet to the depths of our bodies. But alive. Still alive. Parents without any children. But still with the means and the heart to make some more.'

'To save you both,' said Tamburlaine in awe. 'To save you both,' he repeated, 'Caesar gave himself to the owl. He made himself a sacrifice.'

'In those days,' said Michaelmas, 'we still called the beast a bird. That night, after Caesar died, I thought of the thing as a pestilence.'

14
A Trip to the Kitchen

June came to an end that year with a flurry of rain, and the soldiers billeted in the rectory, as trained and expert as British troops are ever likely to be, departed for Flanders. Over there, in French and Belgian mud, they fought bravely, and many died, noble and terrified, in the second battle of Loos. The sergeant was one of the last to go. He was a born survivor, veteran of the Sudan and Spion Kop. But even he fell at last, face to the Germans, in the hail of machine-gun fire at Mametz Wood.

The mice knew, because his death was reported in the papers, and Grandfather Mouse, that doyen of research, discovered a cutting which said that he'd won a medal for bravery.

It began to be a hard war, and a real war. In Norfolk there were shortages of potatoes, and the economies of patriotism affected the natural wastage of cheese and fruit at the rectory. The mice had a rougher time of it, as

Grandfather Mouse had predicted they would.

From day to day, the raids on the larder became less profitable and the mice were more and more inclined to make risky forays on their own. It was on one such foray, albeit undertaken with another object than food in view, that Amelia Mouse came face to face with the enemy, and in a more direct form than Tamburlaine had done.

The soldiers had left Oby in fine style, with drums beating and bugles blowing, and the whole household turned out on the steps to wave them off. They marched down the winding road to Acle with a good British round of cheering in their ears and the rector and his family went back indoors to their evening prayers.

For months the barns were empty and the sounds of bayonet practice were heard no more from the meadow. The leaves darkened on the sycamores and the wind started to rise and then October came, with its bursting chestnut cases and its ripening of walnuts, and then November, with the long drift of rust and gold from the beeches and the ancient elms.

Amelia Mouse was very fond of autumn. Every year she rustled through the fallen leaves with a lift in her spirits. She would roll and tumble under piles of crisp and crackling cornflakes from oak and lime-tree and her twitching nose would inhale the wonderful dank scent of the end of the year.

The very decadence of the season seemed to make her feel young again, and she became quite skittish in her afternoon patrols. This particular year she had an extra reason for enjoying the autumn. Christmas presents, as she'd come to know to her cost, were always a nuisance to think about at the last moment when you'd begun to be busy with getting your Christmas dinner ready. It usually paid to have thought your presents out well in ¹vance.

Amelia Mouse had decided this year to make a start while most mice were still thinking about how to avoid the fireworks and the bonfire on Guy Fawkes night. And she'd hit on a splendid idea for what to give Boadicea. She was going to make her a beautiful doll's house.

She was going to have an acorn cup at each corner of the roof and a magnificent pinnacle of an empty beech-nut case in the middle and the base, the building proper, well, that was going to be a matchbox.

'Three o'clock,' Amelia Mouse said to herself, glancing up at the sun slanting away over the pig-shed at the farm. 'I think there may just be time to get what I need from the kitchen.'

Amelia Mouse brushed down her fur and scampered quickly through the corridors behind the skirting boards to the bathroom. She climbed up the sides of the brick and took a dive and a thorough bath in the baking tin. She wanted to be quite sure that there was no chance of her scent giving away her presence to the servants.

Tingling all over, and feeling quite invisible, as it were, she scuttled through the tiled hall, dodged round the open glass door to the stone hall beyond the front door and then squeezed under a minute space in the Chinese panel that faced the baize double doors to the back of the house.

Amelia Mouse dropped lightly down the three uncarpeted wooden steps that turned past the closed door of the butler's pantry, and then stooped and ducked under the low lintel of a gap in the skirting board, and was suddenly warm and sneezing in the dusty, hot corridor that led directly into the inglenook beside the bread oven.

She took a deep breath and poked her nose out. It was a comfortable, Edwardian scene that confronted her bright eyes. At the broad pine table in the middle of the

room the cook was kneading dough, her sleeves rolled up above muscular reddened elbows. Behind her, on the oak dresser with its array of Jackson's tea tins, jars of raisins and nuts and simple blue china, there was a tray of steaming jam tarts clearly fresh from the oven for tea.

At a table by the window the chambermaid was bending over an enamel bowl, peeling potatoes. Beside the open door of the stove, warming his hands at the cheerful blaze of coke, the coachman was taking his ease in a Windsor chair.

All this Amelia Mouse took in at a glance. Her eye travelled up to the protruding mantel with its carved ends in the form of lions' mouths. The cats had been known to squat high up there and wait for the unwary. But not today.

Amelia Mouse glanced down at the brick floor of the inglenook to left and right. There were two hods of coke, a pair of toasting forks, a shovel, a long riddling-iron and, yes, exactly what she wanted: a crisp, clean box of Captain Webb matches.

'Now,' said Amelia Mouse to herself, and she began to inch her way, very slowly and carefully, towards the box.

She had her little claws on the raw edge of the sandpaper when there was a sudden jerking grind and the kitchen door flew open a foot away from Amelia Mouse's face. She shrank back against the wall of the stove, fearing the worst.

But it wasn't one of the cats questing for prey. It was the lofty, benevolent figure of the rector, radiating good spirits and with one well-scrubbed hand fingering his watch-chain.

'Forgive me, cook,' he said. 'Do you mind if I come in?'

15
The Prisoner

There was a sudden scraping and creaking of wood as the coachman rose quickly to his feet and stuffed his shirt back under his leather belt, from which it had begun to bulge forth as he lounged by the stove. The maid turned from her bowl, made a half-curtsey and wiped her hands on her apron. The cook stood back from the table and looked round rather wildly for something to scrape the dough from her fingers on. The household wasn't used to such an unexpected intrusion on the rector's part into their private domain, and they gave every sign of confusion and surprise.

'Please don't disturb yourselves,' the rector insisted with a broad rather bland smile and a downward sweep of his ample hand.

He looked, Amelia thought, as she froze with her paws on the matchbox, very much as if he was enjoying this kitchen evidence of the awe and respect with which his appearance was being greeted. She kept absolutely

still, not daring to move a whisker, as the rector
advanced into the room.

Having done so, and taken his stand with one hand
on the rim of the oak dresser by the wall, the rector
beckoned towards someone as yet out of sight who had
evidently followed him along the corridor and was
waiting to be invited in.

'I want you,' he said, with a pulpit flourish of bony
fingers, 'to meet Mr Fritz Keitel.'

This introduction was very much in the style the
rector used to present rather important local dignitaries
to each other in the icy grandeur of his drawing room
after morning service, or before evening prayers. But
the crumpled, short, rather hangdog and badgered-
looking man who now appeared in the doorway scarcely
seemed to merit such a grandiose form of words. He
was dressed in the field grey of a German infantry
soldier, wore a red cross armband just above his elbow
and was twisting something evidently designed to go on
his cropped head, and looking very much like a battered
pork pie, in his broad and powerful hands.

'Mr Keitel,' the rector continued, 'is a prisoner of war.
He is being detained, as it were, at His Majesty's
pleasure, at a camp on the outskirts of Caister. By
arrangement with the camp superintendent, my friend
Captain Vickers, and for reasons of good conduct, Mr
Keitel is being allowed off bounds on a daily basis to do
work in the rectory garden.'

At this point, the maid started and put a hand to her
mouth. Amelia felt a tremble run through her fragile
body. She feared that she'd been seen and that there was
about to be a scream, a lifting of skirts above Lisle-
stockinged ankles and then a lunge forward with boots
or broom. But no. Mercifully it was just a hiccup that

had caused the maid to draw in her breath, or perhaps, more probably, a sudden start at the thought of having to confront a German.

'Mary,' said the rector, fixing her with his eye. 'You will see to it that Mr Keitel is given some bread and cheese, and perhaps a bowl of cook's excellent lentil soup. In general he is to have his meal a little earlier than this, in the middle of his working day. But today is an exception.'

The rector watched as a large hunk of bread was set on the table, together with a knife, a spoon and a round board of Cheddar cheese. The prisoner looked up doubtfully at the rector, and was invited, with a wave of the pastoral hand, to pull up a chair and eat.

'Mr Keitel was a builder's mate in civilian life,' the rector continued, 'and he will be working doing repairs

in the formal garden and on the steps to the terrace. You
will see to it, Barker, that he is given access to such tools
and materials as he may require.'

The coachman, thus addressed by his surname,
gulped and nodded. He shifted from one foot to the
other, guiltily aware that he ought, at this hour, to be out
in the stable grooming the mare.

'There will be no need,' the rector was continuing,
'for Mr Keitel to have a bed of his own. He will be
escorted here from the camp in the morning and
collected, as he came, from the front gate at five o'clock.
You will see to it, Mrs Barker, that someone waits with
him in the road until the military transport vehicle
approaches.'

This time the cook nodded, although with a hint of
displeasure. She didn't really see that it was any of her
business to have to make arrangements to supervise
people's arrivals and departures. But the rector was
notoriously eccentric about handing out his instructions
to members of the domestic staff. The servants, in
general, were inclined to listen, agree and to some
extent disobey, or at least reallocate the orders so
inexpertly issued to them.

'I may add,' said the rector, placing the tips of his
fingers together and frowning down at them, 'that in all
respects Mr Keitel will be treated as an equal amongst
you, and accorded all the kindness and decent feeling
appropriate to one from a foreign land who has had the
misfortune to become a prisoner of war.'

By now the object of this harangue was tucking with
hearty appetite into the solid food set before him. He
sucked soup noisily into his mouth and was dipping his
bread in and out of the bowl with a splashy enthusiasm.
Mrs Barker was watching with less placid good will than

the rector, but she forebore to make any comment.

Amelia Mouse began to relax her muscles. As far as she could tell, no one in the kitchen seemed immediately likely to look down and catch sight of her. The rector's monologue demanded attention and the servants were pretending to be all ears. The maid had folded her arms, the coachman had buttoned his jacket and was tentatively holding his lapels. Mrs Barker had put on her pew look, an expression of soulful apathy, as Grandfather Mouse had once referred to it.

'I am not in favour of recrimination or rancour,' the rector concluded, after a lengthy ten minutes of dissertation on the evils of war and the supposed atrocities of the German troops in Belgium. 'It is our Christian duty to love our enemies, and I shall see to it that Mr Keitel is the beneficiary of that love in my house. Have you any questions?'

There was a brief silence punctuated by chewing, and then Barker plucked up his courage to ask what was in all their minds.

'Sir,' he said thoughtfully. 'Do Fritz here speak any English like?'

It seemed to Amelia Mouse, now diffidently edging her prize gently back along the firebricks, to be a momentous question and one very likely to affect the reception the newcomer would get in the household. She watched as the rector nodded sagely, and was clearly preparing to make some considered reply. But it was another voice that now spoke out loud and clear.

'Haff you some peppers, pliss?' it asked in a heavily accented but perfectly intelligible brand of English.

'Very good,' said the rector indulgently, laying his hand as if giving a blessing on Fritz's shoulder. 'Very good indeed.'

Mrs Barker's response was more practical. She turned to the cupboard behind her and brought out a cardboard container.

'Colman's *British* pepper,' she said severely, slapping it down on the pine so that a quantity of grey dusty powder shook up into the air.

Amelia Mouse felt her whiskers tremble in anticipation. She tugged more strongly at the sliding matchbox. Only a foot to go now before she could whisk it out of sight through the hole in the wall. But she was beginning to have an insane desire to sneeze.

'I thank you please,' Fritz said, rising half to his feet and making a sort of curt bow.

Then he slumped back in his place and shook pepper very generously into his soup.

'Atishoo,' said the maid from her place by the window, whisking a dazzling handkerchief from her sleeve and applying it with alacrity to her pretty nose. 'Atishoo. Atishoo. Atishoo.'

Barker had come forward and seized this opportunity to put his arm round Mary's heaving shoulders, a thing he had wanted to do for many a month, Mrs Barker was pursing her lips in a grim disapproval while the rector drew one finger gracefully along the side of his nose. There was bustle, disarray and distraction. It seemed to Amelia that it was now or never.

With a strong tug, causing the wood to bump and grind on the scattered fragments of coal dust, she dragged the base of her future doll's house bodily through the opening in the brickwork and lay back, heart pounding with fear and relief, out of sight and reach behind the wall.

'Mr Keitel,' she heard the rector saying, muffled by the intervening bricks, 'will start work in earnest tomorrow. You might like to spend the remainder of today, Barker, in showing him round the property. That's to say, of course, when he's finished his meal. So good afternoon to you all.'

There was a chorus of deferential farewells, then Amelia Mouse heard the door close and an instant flurry of chatter and recommencement of activity. She rested a moment, half closing her eyes in the blissful darkness. She let her tail rasp on the lovely rough edge where the matches were sparked. She began to daydream of the towering domes and spire as they would be when they were completed. Then she came to reality with a start.

'Right, Fritz,' she heard the hard voice of Barker saying through the wall. 'You can't sit idling here all day, you know. Eat up, and let's begin our tour.'

It was time, Amelia Mouse decided, to return to the rafters with her prize and her news.

16
A Dream Comes True

Snow fell in early December and the notorious bell above the back door tolled with a clapper rimmed with icicles. Every morning the mice watched Mary come out in her apron and hood and pull at the frosted rope with chilblained fingers.

The echoes rolled over a white world of fields hard as iron and water clear as glass, a world where birds hunched in the evergreens with their beaks tucked under their icy wings and where the breath of cattle made visible clouds in the crisp air.

The tolling brought the coachman stamping up the drive from the carriage house, his gauntleted hands beating against his sides for warmth. It drew the odd-job boy up the road to Oby from the village of Thurne, whistling a melancholy tune and occasionally pausing in his dragging walk to make a snowball and hurl it into the crystal tracery in the oak trees.

It heralded, too, the arrival of the prisoner of war, as

the rector had decided he would like to see an earlier
start made each day on the re-laying of the steps to his
terrace. Winter, in the rector's view, made little
difference to the labours of the day. If snow had to be
shovelled aside before stone could be cemented in
place, well, so it had to be. Such difficulties were the
stuff of life.

So the mice would sip their warm morning syrup and
nibble their toasted cheese and listen for the groaning
roar of the transport van from the camp at Caister.
Promptly at seven, it would grind to a halt outside the
iron gates and the stocky, pork-pie-hatted figure of Fritz
would climb down, wave goodbye and stump up to the
door.

'The rector evidently has considerable influence,' said
Grandfather Mouse one day as he gnawed a haunch of
walnut. 'It isn't everybody, you may be sure, who can
get an able-bodied slave delivered to his door every day
by the military authorities. Much may have changed in
this war of theirs, but the Church is still in its old
established position.'

Nobody dared to disagree with this, and the mice
watched Fritz pass in each day to his unscheduled mug
of tea and plate of bread and dripping before his day's
work in the freezing cold began.

It seemed clear enough that the prisoner of war had
soon settled down and was generally liked by the rest of
the servants. He was a quiet, jolly soul and a hard
worker, and he did what he was told without complaint
or laziness.

Mrs Barker, indeed, made quite a favourite of him,
and one day Tamburlaine reported that he'd seen her
bearing a cup of scalding soup out to Mr Keitel in
person, a scarf wound round her ample neck and the

precious vessel carefully clasped in both her well-mittened hands. This kind of personal service was unknown to the gardener.

But the prisoner had accepted the cup as if it were something he was entitled to, so Tamburlaine claimed, and had exchanged a word or two with Mrs Barker, leaning back on a frosted urn and laying his trowel aside in the banked snow.

It began to seem as if Fritz Keitel had made his peace with the enemy and been accepted as a proper and respectable member of the English lower orders. Indeed, it seemed as if he went further than his fellow servants in obedience, never in any way transgressing the written or unwritten rules of the household.

Abroad, in France, the first gas attacks were being made in the Loos salient and the choking fumes were accentuating the gradual realization that the British and German armies were locked in total war. At home, here in Oby, it looked as if the Hun had been tamed, the Teuton industry subdued to the quiet demands of peace.

It was Boadicea who discovered otherwise. In general, it should be said, the little mice enjoyed the run of the rafters and roamed freely over its whole extent without let or hindrance. The space involved was considerable, and divided into many areas, as the joists covered the various rambling rooms and corridors that spread out in all directions below.

Grandfather Mouse had his comfortable home in a group of Crawford's biscuit tins by the south-west corner, above the rector's bedroom. Uncle Trinity and his family lived in their sweetly scented cigar boxes near to the nursery, and Michaelmas and Amelia Mouse lived with the children to the north-east above the bell.

They were simple mice and their favoured rooms were cardboard boxes.

In the middle of the rafters the main landmark was the central chimney breast, and the area beyond this led to the only part of the roof where strict security had to be imposed. This was the low-lying space for several feet on all sides of the hatch, the one entrance which gave access to the roof from the house.

Occasionally a trapdoor would suddenly rise, disturbing a cloud of dust, and a torso would appear framed in the gap, weirdly illuminated by the glow of an upheld candle in a tin holder. At such times, which were unfortunately unpredictable, any sighting of a mouse would have been likely to bring immediate chaos and interference to the rafters.

And so the little mice were forbidden to play anywhere near the hatch. On the whole they didn't. But sometimes the piles of leather suitcases and Saratoga trunks, wonderfully supplied with loose hinges and straps to hang on to and fraying threads to chew, were simply too much for their mouse patience, and they gave way and secretly indulged themselves in frantic and delicious hide and seek in a whirl of squeaking and scurry.

This wasn't what Boadicea had in mind today. She'd crept over on her own, dreaming of Christmas and wondering what her mother and father might have secretly hidden away to give her. She had a shrewd idea of what Amelia Mouse might be making and, well, if accidentally on purpose she just happened to tumble upon something she shouldn't really have seen yet, oh, surely nobody could blame her for that?

The human storage of trunks and boxes covered an area of about a dozen feet, and it offered a splendid opportunity to anyone needing to conceal a special surprise from prying eyes. Of course, it wasn't that Boadicea was really searching, no, not really, not properly, but somehow her little neat feet did seem to have drawn her nearer and nearer to the hatch and its surrounding hiding places.

As always with Boadicea, the search, as it were, for the hidden Christmas present merged in her mind with a highly coloured fantasy touching on the adventures of her favourite white rat, Eric. Boadicea knew, of course, or guessed, that her mother was going to provide her with the doll's house she so particularly wanted. In her fantasies this doll's house took on a wonderful life of its own, springing up with tile-hung gables, conifer-lined driveways and Christmas lights glimmering through long leaded windows.

Towards this comfortable Tudor mansion, jingling with sleigh-bells across crisp and even snow, there advanced in a gathering winter twilight a magnificent reindeer-drawn carriage. Boadicea could hear the gushing sound of runners on snow, the clink of harness, the occasional snap and crinkle of the postillion's whip and now, look, on the front seat, a heavy travelling rug pulled up over his elegant knees, there lounged in a long fine ermine wrap the dangerous and eligible Marquis of Ilfracombe, Lord Rat of Wrathbone.

As the sleigh drew up outside the fine old Gothic doors and the butler came forward with welcoming arms into the falling snow, framing the coy and yet expectant outline of Lady Boadicea of Bude in her Elizabethan hall, heigh ho, with a leap and a flourish of his high feathered hat, down swept Lord Rat, ermine white on white, in the driven purity that fell from heaven.

'Kommst du hier,' said a low, guttural whisper.

Boadicea jumped almost into the air. In a trice her fantasy snapped out of sight. All unbeknownst to her, as she daydreamed, the trapdoor had slowly risen from the floor and there, in a chink of dim light from below, she could see a frowning, gentle face peering out through the piled-up suitcases.

'Mein Kind,' said the whisper again. 'My little one.'

This time the source of the whisper was clear enough, and the sound was accompanied by the staggering advance of a pudgy, dry-cement-coated hand, moving on the dusty floor of the rafters like an enormous five-legged spider.

Boadicea crouched as still as she could. She was only two feet away from the fingers, but she wasn't sure if the man could see her in the poor light, or indeed if he'd really seen her already. Perhaps, despite his whispered instruction, he was just wondering if there was anything there he could tempt out of hiding.

There was nothing for it but to wait and to take her chance with a quick run into the cases if she was really spotted. And then, before Boadicea's astonished gaze, solving the problem and creating a new and infinitely more amazing one, there stepped out from behind a small attaché case none other than the Marquis of Ilfracombe in person.

Admittedly there was no sign of the sleigh or the reindeer but there he was, white as the driven snow, with glinting pink eyes, a long rope-like tail and whiskers as brilliant as the icicles on the bell.

'Mein Johann, my little one,' repeated the whisper, thick with reassured satisfaction this time. 'Du bist mein Freund, my little friend.'

At each of these endearments, Lord Rat of Wrathbone,

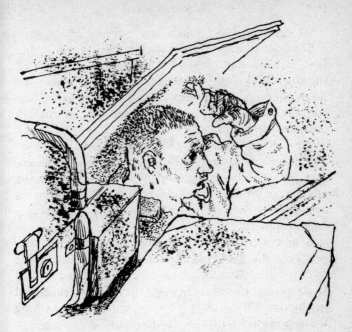

if indeed it was he, inched forward with more assurance. The hand reached up and stroked his enormous, bristling neck. He turned, arching himself.

And then suddenly another hand appeared, and Lord Rat was being lifted, cradled in cupped hands, down and out into the house. There was a sound of more endearments, followed by a quiet crunching and a delicious scent of fresh Cheshire.

But Boadicea waited for no more. She had no desire to be present when the hands returned, and Lord Rat was restored to his hiding place. There was no time to lose. A fantasy rat in her mind was one thing, a real rat in the rafters, and one being fed and cosseted by a human being there, was quite another.

Boadicea ran home as fast as she could.

17
A Council of War

'I saw it,' said Boadicea. 'As clear as daylight. With my own eyes.'

It was the second time she'd recounted the story of how her dream had become reality in the shadow of the leather cases beside the hatch. The first time she'd blurted it out full speed to Michaelmas, breathless from her scurrying along the main joist back home to her family and safety.

Amelia Mouse had poured her a cup of acorn tea and then Boadicea settled down on a bed of feathers to recover her strength and her balance. Michaelmas had listened carefully while she outlined the details, and then he and Boadicea had gone round to collect Grandfather Mouse, who was taking a quiet afternoon sleep.

All three of them – Grandfather Mouse at once alert and wide awake at the thought of trouble – had returned to where Boadicea had been when she saw the hatch open and the rat appear from his hideout.

For several minutes they'd watched and waited. They'd sniffed the air and all agreed that there was certainly a ratty odour about the place. But there was no sign of the creature's presence.

'He's obviously still away with his master,' said Grandfather Mouse. 'We'd better look around while we've a chance of doing so undisturbed.'

So the three mice had scuttled out and begun to make a methodical search for anything the white rat might have left behind amidst the piled-up suitcases and trunks. Unfortunately it wasn't easy to make a complete check. The further they went into the tottering corridors of cardboard and leather, with their occasional open piles of magazines and newspapers, the more clearly it appeared that the whole area was a positive labyrinth.

Once, indeed, poor Boadicea got thoroughly lost, and found herself poised under a huge metal travelling trunk, staring up at an unfastened clasp and wondering where on earth she could be. There were no obvious landmarks amongst the cases, and she wasn't at all sure for a moment which way she ought to turn.

Casting security to the winds, she let out a plaintive little squeak. At once, there was the flutter and scurry of tiny feet, and a pair of quivering ears loomed into view around the corner of an old shoe box.

'Be quiet,' said Grandfather Mouse very severely. 'Do you want the rat to come and eat you up?'

In fact, there was really no danger of this as Boadicea well knew. The mice had no enemies in the rodent world, and their relations with other animals of their kind, large and small, were normally excellent. Even a strange rogue rat in the attic was hardly likely to be a threat to life and limb. It was his impact on the general economy of the household that was worrying.

However, it was obvious that signs of the rat's presence, by way of a den arranged in some corner of a packing-case, or the remains of a meal of cheese or berries, were not after all going to be laid out for everyone to see. And it looked rather as if Boadicea stood a real risk of getting lost and frightened enough to do something silly, like climbing up onto a badly balanced heap of boxes to find out where she was, and perhaps tumbling down and breaking a leg. So the two older mice decided to call off the search and go home for a council of war.

They were all gathered in the drawing room of Grandfather Mouse's mansion, a tall square Crawford's biscuit tin with a fine sheet of decorated cardboard for a ceiling. One wall had been pasted with a good quality Camp Coffee label, and the Scottish soldier being served by his Indian bearer frowned down on the ensuing proceedings.

Both families were present in full. Uncle Trinity had waddled over from his granary, where he'd been doing a stocktaking of hazelnuts, and with him had come his lumpish daughter, Gioconda, and his rather shrewish wife, Ermintrude. With Michaelmas and Amelia Mouse, their two children and Grandfather Mouse himself, presiding in his Four Square tobacco tin armchair, this made a total of eight, the complete population of the rafters.

'What a thing to happen just before Christmas!' Ermintrude was lamenting and Gioconda made a tut-tutting noise to agree with her.

Amelia Mouse rather agreed with both of them, but for different reasons. She got very bored with her relations, and the only time they all tended to come together was indeed for the celebration of Christmas. It seemed a pity, she was reflecting, that this year the annual meeting had had to start even earlier than usual.

But she was a polite and diplomatic mouse, and she had disguised her feelings enough to pour them all out a glass of rosehip wine on Grandfather Mouse's instructions. They were all sipping, and Uncle Trinity's wife and daughter were admiring their reflections in the enormous, magnificent tin walls. It was a bit like attending a dancing class, Amelia Mouse had been known to say of a visit to Grandfather Mouse's mansion, all mirrors and vanity and the choreographer holding the floor.

The choreographer, in the shape of Grandfather Mouse, was holding the floor now while Ermintrude and Gioconda preened their whiskers. The children had emptied their mugs of rosehip syrup and were wishing it had had alcohol in it, like the adult kind, but they were sitting still nevertheless and taking care to listen. Grandfather Mouse could be a martinet when he chose and he didn't like being ignored.

'Assuming the rat was really there,' he began.

'Of course he was there,' said Boadicea. 'I saw him.'

'I know you did,' said Grandfather Mouse kindly. 'But you do have a strong imagination, my dear. You can sometimes, you know, see things that the rest of us don't have access to.'

'All right,' said Boadicea rather huffily. 'I'm sorry.'

Amelia Mouse broke gently in with her usual blandness. 'It's an excellent thing to be blessed with a strong imagination,' she said, reaching over to put her paw on Boadicea's shoulder. 'Your Grandfather admires you for it. One day you'll be the poet of the family, and record our history.'

Grandfather Mouse, who was a vain old fellow in his

way, rather liked the sound of this. He pursed his lips and preened himself. 'A fine idea,' he said. 'I'll think of a title for it.'

'The rat,' said Michaelmas grimly at this point. He was growing irritated by these diversions. 'The rat,' he continued, 'will do us no harm. At least, not personally. We've all met water-rats in the river, and they've all been minding their own business and let us alone. I can't believe this newcomer will be any exception.'

'He'll not be a water-rat,' said Uncle Trinity in his husky wheeze. 'He's a pet rat. Brought in and being looked after, if Boadicea's right, by this German prisoner of war. We've not had much experience of pet rats.'

'German pet rats,' added Ermintrude with a shudder. 'Ughh!'

'What's wrong with a German pet rat?' asked Amelia

Mouse, annoyed by this evidence of a prejudice. 'It's just a rodent like the rest of us, isn't it?'

'Fed on sauerkraut and saluting the Kaiser,' said Ermintrude. 'That's quite enough for me.'

'It won't be a German rat,' said Grandfather Mouse, shaking his head. 'The prisoner wouldn't have been allowed to keep it. The military authorities will have searched each man most carefully and, I'm afraid, confiscated all his personal belongings.'

'Quite right,' said Michaelmas. 'It's obviously a British rat that the prisoner has befriended and made into a pet.'

'He spoke to it in German,' said Boadicea. 'Sounded like German anyway. Some sort of funny language.'

'You don't know any German,' said Tamburlaine. 'You're ignorant.'

'Stop that and apologize,' said Michaelmas. 'The prisoner spoke in German,' he continued, when the apology had been made and some order restored, 'because that's the language he was born speaking and for him it's still the language of affection. He wanted to show his feelings for the rat. That's why he spoke in German.'

'So we've got a British rat in the attic,' said Grandfather Mouse. 'And it's being fed by a German prisoner of war who's no doubt stealing from the larder to get what he needs.'

'That's where the trouble is going to lie,' wheezed Uncle Trinity.

There was a short silence. Amelia Mouse watched the solid forms of her family, comfortable in the warm room, and then the misty outlines of their reflections, like wintry ghosts on the metal wall. She had a moment's vision of the future, later in this terrible war, when nothing would be left of them here except their insubstantial shadows, echoing forever in the tin.

It was an eerie thought, and she shuddered.

'It means a state of emergency,' said Grandfather Mouse.

'Perhaps,' agreed Uncle Trinity. 'But I think we ought to wait and see what happens for a day or two.'

'Keep watch downstairs, I think,' said Michaelmas. 'Overhear their conversations. We'll know soon enough when they start to notice their cheese going.'

The house was short of cheese which was something not made at the farm. Even with Christmas here, supplies would be limited. Michaelmas remembered the last mouse foray to gain provisions. They had only found one drum of Cheddar in reserve and a small pound jar of Stilton. There was going to be trouble if the prisoner started to steal enough to feed a rat.

'We could speak to the rat,' suggested Boadicea a little diffidently. 'Perhaps he'd agree to go.'

'No,' said her father sadly. 'It's winter. He's got to eat. He wouldn't survive now if he went outdoors into the snow.'

'We could force him to,' said Tamburlaine. 'There are eight of us. Four men and four girls. We'd win, for sure.'

But Michaelmas very firmly shook his head.

'We don't want a war with any rat,' he said. 'He's a rodent like us, whatever his origins. No mouse has ever gone to battle with his own kind.'

So that was that. The council of war broke up and the mice made arrangements amongst themselves to monitor all the rooms in the house for conversation about the state of the larder.

'We'll wait and see,' said Grandfather Mouse.

But he didn't have to wait long.

18
Rat on the Loose

Monitoring conversations in the house proved a risky business, as all the older mice had known it would. They took turns to be present at human mealtimes, and to maintain a round-the-clock watch on the kitchen and butler's pantry. Uncle Trinity had a narrow escape from the cats in the game larder, and Michaelmas was trapped for hours behind the last scraps of firewood in a coal scuttle.

The rules for the younger mice going downstairs had to be relaxed, and they too played their part in the eavesdropping. Beyond the rectory, the east winds and the low temperature brought more snow to Norfolk. Beyond Norfolk, in the North Sea, the British fleet – the largest and most magnificent but no longer perhaps the most efficient in the world – patrolled the dark waters and ensured the national lifelines against submarines and blockade.

In Flanders, the advances and withdrawals had come

to an end. The great armies, in khaki and field grey, were already stuck down for their four years in mud. In the air, tiny flying machines fought deadly and sometimes chivalrous battles in the blue, but far below in the trenches there was blindness, choking and self-inflicted wounds.

Three days went by. There were still no signs of the white rat in the rafters, though the female mice had all been searching for him, with a kind of expectant fearfulness, all over the area near to the hatch.

Perhaps he'd been hidden somewhere else. Out of doors maybe, in some nook of the carriage house or the potting shed. Perhaps, and this was Michaelmas's own view though he kept it to himself, the white rat had slipped his traces and was marauding free and uncontrolled in the house.

It was Christmas Day when the awful discovery was made, and it was Grandfather Mouse, on duty in the dining room, who made it. The usual practice of the rector's household on this most auspicious and cele-bratory day of the year, was to rise early, breakfast on cold pork pie and mutton, dress in their best clothes and be off down the winding road to the church of St Edmund the King and Martyr, led by the rector himself, whip and bible in hand, in his gig.

After morning service, a crowded matter of prayers and hymns with a long subsequent flurry of warm handshakings and a brisk return up the road past the schoolhouse in the cold, there was always the grand ritual of Christmas dinner. This was served with full pomp and ceremony, with the chambermaid assisted by her young sister, a bony-faced fourteen-year-old, and the coachman done up for the day in black lapels as a temporary butler.

The dinner started, as the mice all knew, promptly at one o'clock, and it had been decided that someone should most definitely be present in case any vital information were to come to light. The lot had fallen on Grandfather Mouse, who had prepared his stomach by a heavy preliminary meal of Edam rind and Gouda pudding, lest his mouth should water too much when the human meal was served.

The ideal place of concealment in the dining room was an odd one, the lofty interior of the rector's 1840s forte piano. It required a cool head and a nimble foot, which Grandfather Mouse fortunately still had, to get there.

The marble clock on the mantelpiece was chiming one as Grandfather Mouse arranged his tail comfortably behind his back against the cat-gut strings and lifted his whiskers tentatively over the edge of the mahogany casing. The room was still empty, though there were sounds of footsteps and voices in the hall.

Peering over the edge, Grandfather Mouse read sideways the name on the ivory panel to his right, Broadwood and Sons, By Appointment to Her Majesty. His eye travelled further down to the serried banks of keys, then up to the leaning stand, where a sheet of sacred music lay ready for an after-dinner song by the rector's elder daughter, who had a fine soprano voice.

Yes, it was odd, Grandfather Mouse reflected, to be hiding in a forte piano, but it was undoubtedly safe. The way up was hazardous, but the piano was absolutely banned to the cats and there would just be time to skip lightly down before the rector's wife flounced up to the revolving stool, shook back her lace cuffs and struck the ivory with her spiky fingers for the Christmas rendition.

The door of the dining room opened. It was held at its

base by the ebony shoulders of an Indian elephant, now alas tuskless and bruised from years in the playroom, but still providing some humble service as a formidable doorstop. The rector entered, hands behind his back, and took his place in front of the crackling fire. Above the clock, his bald head shone in the antique gilded mirror, surmounted by a Bacchic revel in low relief, where a carriage drawn by lions pursued a nymph through a glade.

'A merry Christmas again, my dear,' said the rector, spreading his hands in welcome, as his younger daughter staggered through the door, an enormous woolly horse cradled in her arms. She was followed, and as it were shepherded, by the rector's wife, resplendent in a fine purple dress, tight-waisted in the fashion she had held to since the mid-nineties. Jewels glittered on her fingers and at her throat.

'My dear,' said the rector again more quietly, with a surprising lack of variety of idea.

Grandfather Mouse had withdrawn his whiskers and was crouched down beside a tiny peephole, where a gap in the Moorish fretwork enabled him to gain an uninterrupted view of the room. The other members of the family were arriving and taking their places round the long, damask-laid table.

It was a noble and cheerful sight. The day was a dim and gloomy one and not much light filtered into this east-facing room past the line of yews and the tall bay tree that formed a windbreak outside in the snow. But the sideboards, the mantel and the middle of the table itself were bright with flickering candles, red and white wax in silver sconces, their flames moving and shifting as the family settled in place.

From the picture rail festoons of holly had been hung

and there was a huge bowl of laurustinus on the piano above Grandfather Mouse's head. In front of each place there was a golden cracker, and sprigs of holly had been tucked in the napkin holders that flanked each plate.

At other times it would have warmed Grandfather Mouse's loyal heart to see Christmas being celebrated with such traditional splendour. But not today. There was a war on, with men dying over crusts of bread and mugs of tea, in their ships at Jutland, on their duckboards at Loos. And the war had laid its icy hand, this new winter, between the two races who had lived before in amity in this calming house.

Grandfather Mouse felt stiff and dry. He eased his old bones in the net of wires, carefully, so as not to make any sound. He wanted a drink of milk, something to sustain and refresh him. But he knew he was pinned to his hiding place for the next two hours.

'For what we are about to receive,' said the rector loudly, hands clasped and head bowed over his napkin, 'may we be truly thankful.'

It was a shorter grace than he often used, but appetite had grown keen in the trot up the road from church, and he was anxious, his family knew, to be settled down with his forcemeat and turkey wing. These delicacies, indeed, were now appearing, the huge bird, sizzling on its plate of gravy, floating over heads raised to admire its passage, as the hands of Mr Barker, butler extraordinary, bore it to its cutting-position on a small table set at the rector's side.

'Well done, Barker,' called young Monty insolently, as if the safe arrival of the bird was an occasion for joy mixed with surprise. But he was ignored. The rector rose to carve, and the towering plates were soon being served by Mary and her sister.

There was a general conversation, clashing of knives and forks, the buzz of genial entertainment. Out of the corner of his eye, Grandfather Mouse could see a cat, the lean brindled one, stalking a blackbird in the snow. But no one seemed to care, or notice. They were living for a moment in a charmed circle, outside the reach of the busy war and its servile ministers.

'It's all so false,' thought Grandfather Mouse, watching from his eyrie in the forte piano. 'They're living in a fool's paradise.'

The plum pudding, domed and blazing, with brandy butter and clotted cream to keep it company, had come and gone, wrecked and crumbled to a few raisins on its blue-rimmed platter. The family were taking a brief respite, gathering their strength for tangerines and walnuts, cheese and water biscuits, when the gaunt figure of Barker, suddenly solemn and ominous, bent and whispered something in the rector's ear.

The rectorial visage furrowed into a grim frown, the rectorial chair was pushed back on its scimitar legs.

'Excuse me,' the rector said.

There was a brief hush as he passed through the door with Barker behind him, a crow-like shadow. Then the talk started again, trivial and fast, uncaring about what might have happened. It couldn't be much surely, after all this was Christmas, wasn't it, the season of rejoicing, of good will to all men.

'Not all men,' thought Grandfather Mouse, as he watched the rector go. Not good will to all men. Nor all mice, either. Not this Christmas. Not ever again.

He knew, before the forbidding figure of the rector returned, tall and condemnatory as an Old Testament prophet, what must have happened to bring Barker in with a secret whisper, a private word in the master's ear. At last, what all the mice had feared was about to happen.

Someone had smelled a rat.

'Not that exactly,' said Grandfather Mouse when he reported the scene later on to the assembled mice in the rafters. 'It wasn't a smell. It was worse than that. A jar of Stilton had been completely eaten out. And there was a hole as big as a man's fist in the last round of Cheddar.'

'Of course,' he went on bitterly, 'they never attempted to find out the true reason. The rector just came back to the head of the table, put his hands in his waistcoat pockets and said flatly, "There are mice in the house."'

'Five years of constant care,' said Grandfather Mouse. 'Five years we've been here, and they've never known. And now that miserable German prisoner brings in a

slovenly rat and within a week we're all in danger of our
lives. It's hardly fair.'

'Life often isn't fair,' said Michaelmas. 'You're given
one lucky escape and you think you're safe for ever. And
then the wheel turns and you're back again in the mire.'

Amelia Mouse laid a comforting paw on her
husband's shoulder, gently massaging the rigid muscles
of his neck.

'What did the rector say they should do?' she asked
gently.

Grandfather Mouse didn't answer.

'It means traps,' he said. 'And if traps don't work,
we'll have the cats up here in the rafters. We'll have them
everywhere.'

'Traps,' whispered Gioconda. 'I've never seen a trap.'

'A fine Christmas this is,' moaned Ermintrude, and
for once the other mice were all inclined to agree with
her.

It seemed a grim and frightening day, even to
Tamburlaine with his box of acorn skittles, even to
Boadicea as she played on the floor with her beautiful
matchbox doll's house, its roof of domes and spires
painted with the red and chestnut juice of berries.

Even to Amelia Mouse, that most calm tempered and
reasonable of creatures, it seemed a grim and frightening
day, and the sun set with a cold wind blowing through
the chinks in the rafters.

A rat was on the loose and nothing would be the same
again.

19
The Week of the Traps

The prediction of Grandfather Mouse about the use of traps was soon fulfilled. Not all the young mice, unfortunately, had seen a trap, and they had to be given a crash course of instruction by their elders. But there was no substitute, really, for first-hand information. And so a regular series of accompanied patrols was instituted.

In the course of these patrols, all parts of the house and grounds were visited and the most likely spots for the siting of traps marked down and recorded. Each patrol was under the leadership of an older mouse, male or female, and its membership consisted of at least two younger mice.

The system worked very well in the cold mornings as the year ended, and the young mice were soon as adept as their elders at recognizing and avoiding whatever might be laid to maim, kill or entrap them. The massive wood and iron engines of ruin were found in the most obvious, and also the most unobtrusive, corners.

Amelia Mouse nosed one out loaded with crumbled Stilton at the very door of the butler's pantry. It could hardly have lasted long there, she reflected, with a hungry spaniel going in and out. Another trap, ingeniously covered with a sprig of holly, was unearthed by the side of a broken dustbin near to the coal-shed. A third was found by Michaelmas, baring its parted steel fangs in the rubbish of the apple store.

The different servants each had their own style, it seemed. The chambermaid was fastidious and frugal in her baiting of clean and tidy spring traps amidst the bedrooms. The cook believed in a forthright placing of something large and strong at either door of the kitchen. People were always tripping over these and cursing, which greatly pleased the mice.

The most serious and vicious trap-setter, of course, was the gardener, Humbleside, who fancied himself as a bit of a marksman and affected a proprietary stroll around the grounds with a shotgun under his arm. He would install his cruel gins and teeth-traps all round the shrubbery, believing, as he insisted against all the evidence, that the cheese depredations were the work of intruders from the wood.

'Them be shrew teeth,' he would say, pointing to some tiny scarrings on the skirting board of the game-larder. 'Bound to get him if we sow the traps round the terrace like.'

The rector, a remote commander in chief with his mind on other business, would nod abstractedly and agree. He was a kindly man and disliked this trap-setting, but he had a horror of what he called uncleanness and he identified this rather mystical evil with all members of the rodent family.

So the traps appeared like tiny piles of scrap metal,

peeking through snow, glaring from frosty leafmould, acute and terrifying in cellar and on landing. Only the rafters themselves were so far left alone, probably, thought Grandfather Mouse, because none of the family yet believed that mice had the strength or the wit to climb. But this, in the opinion of Michaelmas, was only a temporary respite.

For a time there were no casualties. The mice went about their business under crisis conditions, but no one was hurt or caught. This was good, of course, from one point of view. But it was bad from another.

'You see,' Grandfather Mouse explained as he led Gioconda and Tamburlaine one day through the twisted elder forest to the east of the house, 'all human beings need a culprit. They want to be able to say to themselves, the shrews were responsible, or the voles, or the water-rats. And that means they want evidence in the traps.'

Grandfather Mouse made a slitting motion across his throat, raising a curled, soft paw.

'A carcase,' he said quietly. 'A rodent's head on the block. As soon as they catch something, the traps will start to disappear. You mark my words.'

'Well, let's hope it's not one of us,' Gioconda said, with a shiver.

'A sacrifice,' continued Grandfather Mouse, turning over a rigid heap of beech leaves, each edged with its iron rim of frost. 'That's what they need.'

Grandfather Mouse was right, in a way. And the sacrifice came sooner than might have been expected. But its consequences were unexpected, and they forced the war with the human beings one stage further on.

One evening, a patrol commanded by Uncle Trinity, with Tamburlaine and Boadicea as its members, was making a routine check on the stables. This area was well away from the house and it represented only a limited danger to the mice. They normally steered well clear of the horses, anyway, which they regarded as clumsy and hysterical animals, always liable to shy and whinny at the slightest noise.

There were three horses, kept in wooden stalls, under a thatched roof, with stone mangers and iron baskets for their fodder. The black stallion, Mercury, was getting old and a bit weak in the hocks. The mare, Angeline, was a fine, heavy chestnut mare, and there was a beautiful ten-month-old foal, a little mare the colour of honey, with a long sweep of tangly tail and a lovely white blaze on her forehead.

This little mare was the favourite of the rector's elder daughter and that young lady would often come down in the evening to bring some sugar and to stroke the mare's nose. On this particular evening, there was the glow from an oil lamp in the room where hay was kept behind the stables, and the mice guessed, as they scuttled along at the daughter's heels, taking care to keep just clear of the swishing fur at the brink of her cape, that the coachman was indoors working at his table, perhaps on a girth that needed tightening or polish, or perhaps, and these days that was more likely, on the springing of one of his own traps.

It was a dark, windy night, and the mice paused in the shelter of the hand-pump, as the elder daughter fiddled with the latch of the split doors to the stable.

'Vaseline,' the mice heard her whisper.

It was a stupid name for a horse in Uncle Trinity's opinion and he allowed himself a quiet snort into the acorn cup of loganberry syllabub he'd brought to sustain him on the patrol.

'Vaseline,' the girl repeated. 'Where are you, my love?'

The mice shrank back, as she raised her hurricane lamp, and its arc of light swung to and fro on the flaking walls. Then the girl stepped through the door, and the mice ran quickly after her, ducking into a corner behind a heap of leaves. Above them, towering monsters of heat and stench, champing and rustling on their straw, the three horses chinked and jingled in their boxes.

'My dear sweet little horse,' the girl was saying, leaning her cheek towards the foal's neck.

There was a limit to how close she could get, however, as her hair was done up under a wide straw hat, fastened under her chin with a tight swathe of fawn silk. She stood back a moment, set her lamp down on the brick floor, only a few feet from the mice, who cowered away from the reaching blaze of candle-flame, and then snapped open a minute handbag she was carrying.

'There,' she murmured. 'There, my sweet one. Sweets for a special sweetness. Sugar to make you sweeter still.'

This kind of poetic talk was typical of the younger generation, Uncle Trinity had noted, and he put it down to an overindulgence in some of the worst new anthologies. He preferred the stauncher stuff of Kipling and Henley.

But these literary reflections were soon interrupted.

'Miss Esmeralda,' called the voice of Barker from the back room. 'Would you like to come in here, Miss? I've something rather special to show you.'

Esmeralda drew her cape round her shoulders and stepped forward over the low wooden frame into the back room. Behind her, at a signal from Uncle Trinity, who could move rather quickly when he wanted to for such a fat mouse, Tamburlaine and Boadicea scampered over the bricks and straw, keeping well clear of the circle of light, and were peering into the back room at the very moment when Esmeralda bent over what Barker had laid out for her to see on his table.

It was a weird, ghastly scene. The tapering oil-lamp on the scrubbed elm threw a fine, calm glow over the whitewashed walls, and up to the cobwebby remoteness of the sloping rafters, where bats and even owls had been known to roost. The room was empty except for the table and a straight-backed church seat at which Barker, exultant and smiling, was seated in his waistcoat, his shirt sleeves rolled up despite the cold and his feet resting on the rim of a paraffin heater.

Esmeralda screamed.

It was a thin, almost frolicking sound in the confined space, and it set the horses next door to neighing and stamping their hooves. What had caused the girl to scream was not at first apparent to the three mice in the doorway. But then the girl was screaming again, though it was more of a disgusted yelp this time, and her mittened fingers were in her mouth as she backed away against the wall and, yes, there was Barker on his feet now, full height, his shadow distorted and hideous across her body, as he lifted his right hand and dangled, white and bloody in front of her face, the corpse of Fritz Keitel's white pet, the Marquis of Ilfracombe in person.

'Take it away, you foul man,' Esmeralda said, shuddering, as she recovered her voice and something of her poise.

'Why, I'm sorry, Miss,' said Barker, who didn't look to the mice as if he was a bit sorry.

He had an insolent smile on his face, and he was swinging the dead rat to and fro.

'Your father'll be very pleased to see this old fellow dead,' he said, with a grim satisfaction. 'I got him in the game-larder, in a simple spring trap. He was half dead with shock.'

Esmeralda turned her face away, in distaste.

'I gave him his quietus like with a carving-knife,' pursued Barker, tossing the corpse back indifferently on the table, where it lay curled up in a foetus-shape, as if about to be born. 'I never thought we'd have rats, mind you. Mice is one thing, rats are a different story.'

Esmeralda had gone over to the table and was gazing down at the white corpse.

'Poor thing,' she murmured. 'It looks so vulnerable.'

Barker gave a short, coarse laugh.

'Poor thing,' he scoffed. 'They're vermin. The whole ruddy lot of them, if you'll forgive the expression, Miss.'

'I won't,' said Esmeralda, with a warning glance.

Barker shrugged and sat down, putting his feet back on the heater.

Esmeralda was still looking down at the rat.

'Goodnight, Barker,' she said suddenly. 'I'll tell my father what you've done. I'm sure he'll be very pleased.'

Then she turned and, with a swish of her cape, was gone. The three mice looked at each other, watching the bobbing glimmer of her hurricane lamp as she walked back to the house in the wind.

'So much for your white rat, Boadicea,' said Uncle Trinity.

'So much for the Marquis of Ilfracombe,' said Boadicea to herself.

And Lord Rat of Wrathbone was already enjoying a most sumptuous funeral in her mind as the three mice scampered back along the icy cobbles to tell the others their news.

20
The Cats in the Rafters

Upstairs, in the rafters, it was Michaelmas who drew the grim conclusion.

'It's the worst that could have happened,' he said. 'They'll be sure now they've got rats. And rats, they'll believe, can inhabit any part of the house, high or low. It means a war here in the rafters.'

The three older mice were ensconced in Michaelmas's comfortable cardboard study, reclining in their straw chairs, with generous cups of hazel brandy to help their deliberations. Uncle Trinity had sent Boadicea and Tamburlaine off to bed, and had rapidly apprised his brother and father of what they'd seen and heard in the stables.

Grandfather Mouse was now twisting his acorn cup in his paws.

'I'm not sure that I agree with you, Michaelmas,' he said. 'We must still wait and see. The rat was white, after all. Someone may rightly guess that it was being kept as a pet. Who knows? The German prisoner of war may even own up.'

Uncle Trinity shook his head.

'He won't,' he said very positively. 'The man's here on sufferance. He won't risk his job, and the heavy punishment he may anticipate, by raising his voice out of turn. He'll lie low and keep his mouth shut.'

'Of course he will,' agreed Michaelmas. 'Everyone knows how the rector feels about vermin. He thinks that cleanliness is next to godliness and, God help him for it, he believes that all our race is unclean.'

'They deserve a lesson,' said Uncle Trinity, who could be savage on occasion. 'For all this talk about religion, and equality, and right behaviour, the rector's a primitive child at heart.'

It was dark and warm in the cosy frayed cardboard room, and the mice felt relaxed and ready to cope. Amelia Mouse came in softly, filled their cups with more brandy and then slipped unobtrusively out again, pausing only to give her husband's shoulder a loving squeeze as she passed him.

'So what do we do?' said Grandfather Mouse judiciously.

'It's after ten,' said Uncle Trinity with a slight belch. 'I counted the chimes as we came past the marble clock in the hall. That means the rector and his wife will soon be going up to bed. I don't suppose that Esmeralda will mention the rat, or not tonight. She'll be up in her room by now, soothing her troubled mind with a book. As for Barker, he won't be bothered to walk up to the house till morning. He'll be here for his breakfast when he hears that awful bell tolling and then he'll see the rector in his study at eight.'

'So that gives us all night to prepare for a siege,' said Michaelmas.

There was a long silence. Each mouse was busy with his own thoughts. They all knew what Michaelmas had in mind, but they were slow to voice it. At last, Uncle Trinity stirred his bulky fur and put the danger into words.

'You think the rector will have the cats sent up,' he said.

Michaelmas nodded.

'Rats, my dear fellow,' he snorted loudly, mimicking the rector's deep baritone. 'I want action taken at once. You will see to it that the cats are allowed the immediate run of the whole house. Particularly the cellars and the attics. Report to me in the evening on what they've found.'

'Very good, Michaelmas,' said Grandfather Mouse admiringly. 'I always said you ought to have gone on the stage. You've got him to a T.'

'They'll range all day,' mused Uncle Trinity, stroking his whiskers. 'When darkness comes, Barker and the chambermaid will go round and assess the kill.'

'But there won't be any kill,' said Michaelmas quickly. 'Not if we make our preparations right. And there's just a chance they'll call the hunt off if the cats don't find any traces.'

'What do we do?' asked Grandfather Mouse. 'Where can we go?'

'Listen,' said Michaelmas, and he told them.

It took seven hours to reduce the attic to stockade conditions, and that was with all eight mice working full time. The first thing Michaelmas insisted on, was a thorough disinfecting of all the joists and rafters. Uncle Trinity went down with Gioconda and Ermintrude, and they gnawed several long slabs from the block of Lifebuoy soap in the cloakroom. Amelia Mouse and Boadicea made journey after journey to carry up buckets of water from the baking-tin, and Tamburlaine and Michaelmas and Grandfather Mouse hauled over a metal ashtray that had somehow found its way under the eaves.

In Grandfather Mouse's shining hall, they set up a crisis ablution centre. There, one after another, all the mice took a thorough bath, washing from head to foot with more special care than they had ever done before.

'Your lives may depend on this,' Michaelmas told them. 'So don't skimp any corners.'

After the washing, the mice went all over the attic clearing up such derelict heaps of straw or litter as might still retain some odour of their presence. Mercifully, there was very little. They were extremely clean little animals, and the rafters were always kept spick-and-span.

Finally, they closed up all entrances to Uncle Trinity's cigar-box farm and Michaelmas's cardboard house, pushing away the props of wood and stone that enabled their own comings and goings to take place. All that was left, when they'd finished, were two casual piles of old boxes, impregnable even to foot or head of cat. Or so they hoped.

Looking at their homes now, closed and empty, the two brothers felt a pang of sadness. It was the fate of mice to be always on the move, as they both knew, but they'd come to feel settled up here out of the wind and the rain. It was hard to accept this threat to their continuing presence.

'Never mind, Trinity,' said Michaelmas. 'It may only be temporary. Perhaps in a few days we'll be able to open things up again.'

'Of course,' agreed Uncle Trinity, but neither of the brothers really believed it.

Early in the morning, when the first rays of sun began

to creep wintrily through the chinks in the roof, the mice were grouped in a close huddle under the great gleaming cavern of Grandfather Mouse's drawing room. They'd dragged the tray of water and the soap in here, and enough food for several days. The usual doorway had been reduced in height, and only the minute Boadicea could now slide underneath it with ease. The portly Uncle Trinity needed helping paws to push him through from behind.

'Every four hours,' said Michaelmas, when they were all gathered, 'we must all take another complete bath. In relays, and in absolute silence. As long as we're here, we'll keep a regular watch, too, beside the wooden prop. When the sentry gives the order, everyone is to freeze.'

'It all sounds awfully difficult,' wailed Ermintrude. 'Is it really necessary?'

Grandfather Mouse took hold of her by the ears.

'Death,' he said, shaking her up and down. 'That's what it means. Death, if we don't do exactly as Michaelmas says.'

The mice were in position by eight o'clock, and for some hours nothing happened. In fact, it was high noon when the trapdoor was lifted, and the cats, for the first time the mice could remember, came into the attic. Uncle Trinity was on watch.

'Now,' he said simply, hearing the distant creak, and seeing the light flood over the floor.

There were three of them. Katrine, the spayed mother, with her cast eye and her tattered brindled coat. The Black Prince, with her whiskers like sprayed ice, her false name and the ring-worm scar in her forehead. And the Grey Kitten, the biggest of the lot, with his dished flanks like a battle-cruiser and the great open scimitars in his velvety paws.

They made a vicious crew. Hungry, marauding, and insolent. They ruled the back stairs part of the house and most of the garden. Taking whatever they needed from branch or plate or cranny. With no respect or love for man or beast. Only their fawning servility when they wanted a saucer of cream or their back stroked. And underneath, their spitting treacherous mania. The pathological need to kill and torment.

The mice loathed them. They heard them pad and patter now through the world they regarded by right of tenure as their own. They listened with ears pricked and noses quivering, imagining their homes being sniffed over and pawed at, their trails under joist and rafter followed, perhaps, and wondered at.

Further away the pad and pattering went. The sudden leaping and low squeaks and murmurs. Then closer again. Closer. Uncle Trinity shrank back away from the prop. He could smell the terrible feline odour first. Then he saw the sudden darkening of his field of vision. One of them was there, outside the tin.

Tamburlaine felt Boadicea's claws tightening on his paw. He followed her eyes. Below the prop there was a thick line of black and rusty fur. It was just as if someone was trying to thrust a sable hearth rug in through the gap.

A deep growling purring noise began. It seemed to climb up and coil round the ceiling and creep slowly down at the mice. They knew the noise of old. It was the Black Prince's war cry. She purred for everything. When she was happy, or irritated, or frustrated, or even, so Uncle Trinity said, when she was bored.

Outside the tin there was a thud and a gasp. Then a snarling noise and a quick spitting. The cats were divided, as they often were, and fighting. Then the noise stopped, and a set of clattering bones, huge as elephant's tusks to the mice, and as deadly as Japanese swords, came sweeping over the floor to a few inches from where they cowered.

The fur behind them was brindled. They were Katrine's. The mice held still, packed in a soft bunch against the far wall of the tin. The claws were only a mouse length away. Then they swept aside and were gone again through the gap. The cat was tired, or convinced there was nothing there.

The mice relaxed. For an hour or so, the cats prowled to and fro, questing through every part of the rafters, but focusing most of their attention, so far as the mice could tell, on the pile of suitcases and the area around them. It must be the rat's odour, thought Amelia Mouse. It was harder to eradicate than their own. Poor rat, she found herself adding in her mind. It wasn't his fault all this had happened. He'd been alone, and lonely. And he'd died alone. The worst that could happen to anyone.

At last, the sounds of the alien presence became intermittent and the mice knew that the cats were going to and fro between the attic and other, clearly more interesting, parts of the house. Finally, when Grandfather Mouse was on watch, they heard what they all most wanted to hear; the creak and clump and the onset of shadow that indicated the trapdoor had been replaced, and the cats withdrawn.

'They'll be back soon with a lamp, though,' predicted Michaelmas. 'To go over the battlefield.'

He was right. An hour or so later, there was a louder creaking, and the sound of voices. Then the sweep and flicker of a candle-flame, stuck in a low holder and carried over a plump thumb. Boadicea knew that candle. She'd seen it resting beside the chambermaid's truckle-bed, when she'd watched in rapt fascination as that prim young lady removed frilled layer upon layer of starched lace before jumping spryly into her blankets in shift and knee-length bloomers.

Now Boadicea, whose watch it was, saw right up under the massive dome of Mary's dress, where those same intriguing bloomers, or their fellows, were shrouded in rafter shadow. Then the stooping figure moved, and the gaitered legs of the rector himself replaced them, shining and polish-smelling.

'Nothing here, sir,' the voice of the maid was heard saying, after the two had traversed the length and breadth of the attic. 'Not a single tail or whisker to be seen.'

With which judgement, the second phase of the war against the mice came to an end.

21
The Last Weapon

But the rector was a man not easily satisfied, as the mice were soon to find out. Some days went by in a state of odd suspension. There were no more invasions of the attic, and the number of traps in position seemed fewer than before.

Every day the mice took turns to make slow and careful patrols round the house, and every night the information they pooled was the same. Despite the most exacting monitoring of human conversations, both in front of and behind the baize doors, there was no indication of new hostilities.

Nevertheless, Michaelmas was doubtful.

'It's far too early to resume our normal lives,' he said as they held their evening conclaves in the embattled biscuit tin. 'We must wait at least another week.'

So 1915 ended, in a blizzard of sleet and high wind. The Scots doctor from Clippesby drove over at a spanking pace after midnight, with his silver flask of

malt whisky, and his black hair glinting with rain to
ensure good luck for the new year. It was a raw January,
wet and cold and miserable, and the news from France
was appropriately dull and depressing. Only the
successful evacuation of Gallipoli served as a brighter
spark in the uniformly disagreeable pages of the *Daily
Telegraph*.

Nine days of January had gone, and the pressure on
Michaelmas to agree to a return to pre-crisis conditions
was mounting. By the tenth morning he was contem-
plating a relaxation of security.

It was Tamburlaine, breaking rules for a long foray
into the dairy, who proved his caution right. For an
aggressive and energetic adolescent mouse, big and
strong as Tamburlaine had grown to be, it was hard to
accept the restriction of only patrolling in company with
an adult.

There were many parts of the house to cover, and
neither enough mice, nor enough time, to cover them
in. So Tamburlaine waited until his morning off had
come, when the other mice were out on their duties,
and he slipped rapidly and secretly down to the part of
the house he knew to be most dangerous of all, though
probably also the most important to find out about.

The dairy lay beyond the kitchen, and was approached
by a short corridor leading past the laundry room and
the tradesmen's door. It had a door of its own, giving
directly onto the cobbled yard fronting the coal and
wood sheds, and rising to the well under the ash tree.
Nobody knew why the dairy was called the dairy. It may
once have been a room the cows were brought to from
the field to be milked or sheltered in.

But it was more likely that the little high room behind
it had been used to store cheeses in, and the dairy itself

had held stocks of milk and cream. An old butter-churn, derelict in its elm frame, still stood in one corner. But for many years, far exceeding the memory of any local servants, the dairy had been used as a wash-house and scullery, with an increasingly important secondary purpose of providing a sort of parlour where the servants could idle and chat around the great fire-blackened refectory table.

This particular morning, there was a cheerful blaze of beech logs in the huge open grate that ran almost the length of one wall. Busying herself with a pile of washing at the copper, and occasionally pausing to stoke the fire with more wood from a stack above the bread oven, stood the capable figure of Mrs Barker.

When Tamburlaine arrived, wriggling as he loved to do through a narrow aperture behind the mangle, there was a visitor in the dairy, none other than the short, ferrety-faced Humbleside, the gardener. Humbleside, whose appearance always belied his lowly name as if he was deliberately trying to contradict it, was lounging by the open back door. He was wearing high folded-back wellingtons, of the kind affected by shooters and fishermen, and his hands were casually thrust in the deep pockets of his Norfolk jacket, as if they were much too proud to consider any manual labour.

'There was no cover for the advancing columns,' he was saying, in the tone of a man delivering a final and incontrovertible verdict, 'except Lala Baba, on the verge of the sea, and Chocolate Hill. The rest of the way was open plain, with a slight rise, swept by artillery fire.'

Humbleside paused, frowning as though to recall the exact contours of the battlefield at Suvla Bay.

'According to Sir Ian Hamilton,' he continued, 'for a mile and a half there was nothing to conceal a mouse.'

This grim news made the intrepid young Tamburlaine freeze in his tracks. His bright eyes flickered out across the quarry-tiled floor, up the whitewashed walls, right round the beamed roof, and down over press and cupboard, sink and pump, until they rested safely again on the reassuring green and red pierced iron rampart of the immovable sycamore wringer whose protective bastion Tamburlaine was relying on.

Satisfied, Tamburlaine relaxed. At Suvla Bay, evidently, the mice had been less lucky.

'You talk sometimes as if you'd been there yourself,' said Mrs Barker a touch scornfully, as she heaved a rumpled mass of sheets from the copper into the sink.

'I rely, madam, on *The Times History of the War*,' said Humbleside, with dignity. 'Illustrated,' he added.

'You get more of a laugh about it out of *Punch*, I'd say,' said Mrs Barker, squeezing and twisting the sheets into long braids in her hands. 'For example,' she continued, pausing and wiping her hands dry on her apron. 'There was one drawing of a posh lady entertaining a wounded soldier to a cup of tea. "You say the bullet went in at the front of your shoulder," she says, "and came out at the back. Now tell me – I do so want to know – which did you feel the most – when it was going in or coming out?" '

Mrs Barker lifted the burning logs from underneath with a long poker, and watched the flame spurt and crackle, as air flowed in and gave it breath.

'They called that one, "People we should like to see interned," ' she said. 'And I agree. There's too many people in this war gloating and being curious about human suffering and not doing nearly enough to alleviate it and get things brought to peace again.'

Humbleside put on a supercilious smile.

'A poor weak woman like you would hardly understand,' he said blandly. 'This war, like all wars, is a matter for the male animal to put to rights.'

Humbleside strolled over to the fire, and stood with one elbow on the mantelpiece, gazing down reflectively into the flames.

At this point, the door onto the corridor opened, and young Tamburlaine peered sideways through the wheel of the wringer at the shirt-sleeved figure of Barker, who was carrying a saddle under his arm.

Humbleside turned, and nodded a greeting.

'Well,' said Barker, resting his saddle on the table. 'Did you get the stuff?'

The scent of saddle-soap wafted down to Tamburlaine's pricking nostrils, as he climbed up to get a better view through the iron tracery of the wringer's supports.

'I did,' said Humbleside, and there was a low clump as he set something down on the oak, something that

Tamburlaine watched come out of his jacket pocket in his hand, and then lost sight of as it rested above his head, where the rim of the table obscured his vision.

'Lord save me,' said Mrs Barker, coming over to the table.

There was a long silence, broken only by the logs crackling in the grate.

'You'll never,' said Mrs Barker, 'Surely never.'

'The rector himself insisted,' said Humbleside, rather primly. 'You know his opinions about things being clean.'

Barker laughed, a harsh bitter sound.

'You talked him into it,' he said coarsely. 'You devious old rascal. He'd never have gone so far himself, whatever the risks.'

'He wants me to do the cellars and the attic,' said Humbleside, ignoring the tone of this. 'I shall, of course,' he added with a vicious satisfaction, 'carry out his instructions to the letter.'

Mrs Barker had gone back to the copper, and was disguising her feelings in a severe pummelling of pillow-cases. Barker picked up the saddle, and walked over to the outside door.

'You're a cruel devil, Humbleside,' he said over his shoulder. 'You'd exterminate every living thing, if you could, that's wild and free. It's the likes of you that got that mustard gas used on the Western Front.'

Humbleside flushed, and took a step forward. But he let Barker go. The coachman was a head taller than he was, and more than two stone heavier.

'The rector wants to be sure,' he said defensively. 'It's the only way.'

Mrs Barker turned, her face red with suppressed anger.

'It's my belief,' she said firmly, 'that there was just the one rat Willy caught. There's never been rats or mice in this house, or none but one or two come in from the harvest fields, and them don't do any harm to nobody.'

Mrs Barker seized what Humbleside had laid on the table and lifted it high in the air, a sinister cardboard cylinder, with a blue label, and one word in red that was large enough for Tamburlaine to read from the floor, where it made him quake with terror.

'Poison,' said Mrs Barker indignantly. 'It's a sin and a shame to lay that stuff in the house. And a waste of money, and a corruption of human love. Now get you out of my scullery, and take your filthy cardboard box along with you. Rat poison, indeed!'

So this was the last weapon, the terrible news of which it had fallen to young Tamburlaine, scared and quivering, to bring back with him to the rafters.

22
In the Nursery

It was Uncle Trinity who first heard the news. Tamburlaine was scampering along the corridor past the open door of the nursery when he heard a low, coughing grunt, and, putting his nose cautiously round the door, he saw Uncle Trinity lolling half-asleep under the iron bedstead, beside a moth-eaten teddy bear who was wearing a white smock and a fisherman's hat.

Some distance away, gazing in rapt awe through the swung-aside wall of a Gothic doll's house, was Gioconda. What gripped her attention so completely, as Tamburlaine could see, was the tiny swivel mirror in the doll's bedroom, in which the vain little mouse was preening and admiring herself.

'Uncle Trinity,' hissed Tamburlaine, running under the bed and seizing his uncle by the shoulder. 'Wake up! Wake up!'

Uncle Trinity, to do him credit, moved fast. He had rolled his portly bulk to one side, opened his eyes, and backed his rump and tail between the teddy bear's crumpled legs, before Tamburlaine had time to do more than get out the first 'w' of his second 'wake up'.

Nevertheless, Uncle Trinity felt a little discomfited. The two younger children, Monty and Gorgo, whose room this was, were always downstairs for their music lesson at this time in the morning and, indeed, the strains of a poorly executed aria from the *Messiah* picked out on the rector's American harmonium could just be detected filtering up through the floorboards. But it was still a security risk to be dozing for all to hear with his teenage daughter unprotected a few yards away.

So Uncle Trinity took refuge in complaint. He oared himself forward, with the forearm movement fat mice find convenient, and fixed Tamburlaine with his beady eye.

'Tamburlaine,' he said, in a tone of disturbed surprise, as if identifying the intruder for the first time. 'What are you doing here?'

Then he realized that the little mouse was quivering with terror, far more than he might have been if he'd just been caught doing something naughty. Uncle Trinity spoke more gently.

'What's the matter?' he asked.

In the scrap of mirror-glass, sheltered by the painted Gothic of the doll's bedroom, Gioconda stroked her whiskers, and inclined her head, and put her hand on her elegant rump, exactly as if she was a fine lady, or a fashion model, in the heyday of Edwardian elegance. And cowering beside a tray of lead soldiers, with their heads replaced on matchsticks, and their guns bent in tortuous blasts of nursery war, Tamburlaine gulped out the story of what he had heard and seen in the dairy that was going to mean the end of an era for the mice in the

attic, and for Tamburlaine himself, though no one knew it yet, a terrible place in mouse history.

There were many vanities in those far-off days, and Gioconda was the heir to them. One day she and her mother, Ermintrude, had raided the doll's toy cupboard in the nursery and come back to the rafters dressed from nose to tail in the ragged human splendour of doll's house people, with floor-length skirts, and farthingales, and huge straw hats on their tiny heads.

'Look what we've found,' they'd said, entirely full of their own magnificence and glory.

But Grandfather Mouse had read them both a bitter lesson.

'Mice don't wear clothes,' he'd said with utter scorn. 'Those petty gauds are for human beings, who don't know any better. Our beauty lies in our own skins. We *are* our clothes.'

Gioconda and Ermintrude had stripped off their silly finery then and there, and the little clothes had gone straight back into the doll's house, after a thorough wash in carbolic soap, to remove any mousy smell. But they still dreamed of the hats, and the long dresses, and Ermintrude was prone, in her day, to go down with her daughter and stare in joy and wonder at the illustrations in some beautiful little square books the children had, and sometimes left lying open on the floor, by a lady called Beatrix Potter.

Mice once wore clothes, thought Ermintrude, and she said as much to Gioconda, but neither repeated this notion, wisely perhaps, to Grandfather Mouse. He was a mouse who didn't like to be contradicted.

In the back of a small wooden cart, whose off-side wheel had come off and left it with a strange tilt, Uncle Trinity put his face in his paws as he listened to Tamburlaine. He saw the future spread like the pack of cards that Gorgo had scattered over the carpet, suits interspersed with suits and all in chaos.

'Happy families,' thought Uncle Trinity, as he looked at Mr Bun the Baker with his head folded over. 'Yes, we were certainly happy once.'

He felt a surge of rage go through his body.

'Poison,' he said to Tamburlaine. 'You're absolutely sure you saw the word Poison on the box?'

Tamburlaine nodded. 'In red,' he said.

So it was true, thought Uncle Trinity. The rector meant to carry through his war to the end. It wasn't enough to have caught the white rat, the real culprit. He'd tasted blood. He wanted more.

'Uncle Trinity,' said Tamburlaine, a little diffidently. 'How will they use the poison?'

Uncle Trinity came down from the cart. He swung

round and lashed a wooden puppet across the face with his tail. He felt the surge of rage turning to cold fury in him.

'There are ways and ways,' he said.

Uncle Trinity knew the way they would choose, though. It was Humbleside, whom Uncle Trinity had once seen break a mole's back with his cane, who would make the arrangements. Humbleside the vicious. Humbleside the thorough.

There would be no tipping of powder between the joists and along the skirting boards. No smearing of an evil jam along the moulding of door-bottoms and window-frames. Those chancey means would be far too casual for Humbleside.

Uncle Trinity ran his claw, in a savage gesture, along the shiny dining carriage of a toy train. They'd know he'd been there after this.

'Gioconda,' said Uncle Trinity.

His daughter looked round, a minute jar of face cream in her paw.

'Let's go,' said Uncle Trinity.

There was no point in venting his rage in the nursery. After all, they would simply suppose the children had scratched their toys.

'We'll have to evacuate the rafters,' Uncle Trinity said as he and Tamburlaine and Gioconda made their way back up through the staircase in the flue to the attic.

'Why?' asked Tamburlaine. 'I don't see why.'

'They'll smoke us out,' said Uncle Trinity. 'They'll take the whole house, room by room, space by space. Wherever we could live, and that means wherever they don't live themselves, they'll burn that poison and fan a lethal smoke through. I know that man Humbleside. He'll do the barns and the cellars, and finally he'll do the rafters.'

Tamburlaine was thinking.

'We could climb out on the guttering,' he said after a while as they reached the hole out to the attic. 'After a day or two, when the smoke clears, we could make our way back in.'

Uncle Trinity shook his head.

'It lies for weeks,' he said sadly. 'We'd either die of frostbite on the roof or come back in and get lung disease and die choking.'

Gioconda burst into tears.

'I don't want to die,' she wailed. 'I want to grow up and join a circus and wear a frilly dress and dance in the ring.'

'Be quiet,' said Uncle Trinity. 'Don't be so frivolous, girl.'

He was all consumed by rage now. He could feel it eating through his body, like a fungus in rotten wood.

Revenge, he thought.

He repeated the word inside his head and he felt it begin to swing and toll there, like a great bell, filling his mind with its clamour and resonance. Then he realized what he was thinking and a white, savage light dawned in his brain.

'The bell,' he said aloud. 'That's it.'

Revenge was difficult. There were few aspects of life at Oby rectory which the mice could seriously alter by their actions. But at least they could manage a symbolic vengeance. They could make sure that the bell would never ring again.

The bell, like the bell in the church steeple at Thurne, was a thing of power. It swung on high and ruled the comings and goings of many people by its clangour. The mice would bring it crashing to the ground.

23
A Plan for Action

In the safety of the rafters the three mice paused for breath. Some distance ahead of them lay the group of biscuit tins that had once constituted the stately home of Grandfather Mouse and that were now, under stockade conditions, the last refuge of the eight mice in the attic.

Rather slowly, since Uncle Trinity was wheezing and puffing after the climb, they began their walk along the lath and plaster. Above their heads to the left, straight and sparkling as telegraph lines, there ran the wires for the house's internal bell system, a dangerous jungle of strings and creepers that the mice were all absolutely forbidden to go near or touch. A single false note on one of the tiny square boxes in the kitchen, where a red marker jangled to show what room was ringing for service, would very soon have brought a dire retribution, a sure knowledge that there were mice in the roof.

Uncle Trinity looked up at the wires with a mixture of hatred and envy. It would be so easy to leap up and swing on the wires, to confuse, for a few minutes at least, the whole economy and communications system of the house. But he restrained his impulse. The revenge he needed must be of a more permanent kind.

Uncle Trinity turned his eyes to the rising bulk of the main Crawford's biscuit tin, the one whose interior formed the great silver hall of the house. Outside, it presented a splendid façade of purple and gold, a little dented and scratched here and there, but still with a fine image of the late Queen Victoria embossed within an oval frame, and surrounded with the tartan pipes and kilts of a cartouche fit for an empress.

Yes, it had been a noble seat for the head of the house, Uncle Trinity thought, as the three mice bent and squeezed under the low lintel, carefully braced on a slender pencil box. It was a shame to see its outhouses closed and abandoned, and the whole family reduced to moving in under one roof.

Uncle Trinity sneezed, and pulled a wry face. There was still a faint smell of the cats around the doorway, where the Black Prince had lain and stretched her dark shag hide that fateful day of the invasion.

'We're all alone,' said Tamburlaine, returning from a quick foray around the house.

Uncle Trinity nodded. He took a cup of hazel brandy down from a shelf, and served himself a generous measure. In his mind's eye he was seeing the low-lying roofs of his farm, the sweet spread of fragrant cigar-boxes, redolent of cedar and smoke, where he and his wife and child had settled in the south-west corner of the rafters. They were empty now, and defiled by the paws and teeth of the cats.

'Grandfather Mouse will be back soon,' said Uncle Trinity to Gioconda, who was smoothing down her fur in the beautiful reflection of the walls. 'I want you to stay here and tell him what your cousin saw in the dairy.'

Uncle Trinity changed his position.

'Tamburlaine,' he said very quietly. 'I want you to come with me.'

Uncle Trinity took a deep breath. Then, very rapidly, he outlined his plan. 'I'll need your help,' he concluded. 'It's not something I can do alone.'

'Of course not,' said Tamburlaine excitedly. 'Let's go at once.'

Then a surprise note of caution seemed to strike him.

'Perhaps we should wait, though,' he suggested. 'I mean, until my father and mother get back and I can tell them where we're going.'

'They'll know soon enough,' said Uncle Trinity. 'Gioconda will tell them where we've gone. Your father's been at me to do something about that bell for a whole year. He'll be pleased we've made a start.'

At this moment, there was a great surge of noise and the tin began to shake and boom in a low earthquake of sound. The three mice waited in stunned silence, looking at each other.

'Speak of the devil,' said Uncle Trinity as the noise began to fade and echo away.

'But why are they ringing the bell now?' asked Gioconda. 'It's long after breakfast time.'

Uncle Trinity smiled grimly.

'It's their fire drill,' he said. 'It's been rung to gather the whole household together, servants and family, and I think I know the reason why. It's for Humbleside to give out a general warning about the poison. He'll be going to start on the cellars. They won't want any of the children going down and getting choked.'

'So soon,' said Tamburlaine. 'They don't waste any time.'

Uncle Trinity heaved himself to his feet. He flicked his tail up over his shoulder.

'It's the last time that bell will ever ring,' he said, savagely. 'Are you coming?'

Tamburlaine nodded.

Leaving Gioconda behind, a little disconsolate but solaced by a tiny sprig of wild grapes, the two mice set off.

They made their way easily along the rafters to the chimneypiece, and from thence down a twisting channel which led from brick to brick into a dark corner of the chambermaid's bedroom. This room had at some time in the past been divided into two, and the smaller portion was now boarded off to accommodate the two thirty-gallon tanks which served Oby rectory as its tap-water supply.

It was in this smaller area that Uncle Trinity and Tamburlaine now arrived. Above them rose the enormous cylindrical bulk of the lead tanks, two static monsters that stood beaded with moisture in the darkness and rumbled and dripped and gurgled and wheezed like a pair of uneasy stomachs after an unusually heavy meal.

These troubled sounds might have proved a distraction to a member of the family or a distinguished visitor, so the remaining two-thirds of the room had been allocated to that lowest and least important member of the household, Mary, the chambermaid.

The two mice scurried forward and peered through a gap in the boarding to make sure that her room was empty. It was. The brass and iron bed in the corner lay neatly made and tucked in, with a fine silk cover depicting arabs and camels arranged on top.

There was a fireplace with a gilt overmantel, a wash-stand with a flowered jug and bowl, and a tidy pine chest of drawers supporting an oil-lamp with a ruby funnel. Beside this lamp, as Uncle Trinity knew from earlier forays here, there always lay open a grand illustrated bible from which the chambermaid was accustomed to read a few passages each night in her white shift before retiring to sleep.

'Nobody here,' said Uncle Trinity, satisfied with his inspection of the room. 'She's down with the others.'

He led the way through the hole and the two mice ran over the strip of worn but spotless carpet to the window. Making a back for Tamburlaine, Uncle Trinity enabled the younger mouse to scramble up onto the bed-steps and from there to the window-sill. Testing the holds, Tamburlaine came back and stretched out a paw to help Uncle Trinity climb up beside him.

It was an exhausting business, but it was managed. The two mice leaned on the ledge and peered out and across the roofs of the dairy and the coal sheds away towards Ashby Hall in the distance.

There maybe, thought Uncle Trinity. That might be where the mice could find a new home. But he put the thought away. For the moment he had other matters on his mind.

As Uncle Trinity had expected, the casement was on the latch. The chambermaid had the usual English passion for fresh air, and there were few mornings, rain or shine, when the window was kept closed. As it stood now it offered, by a perilous but accessible series of stages, a possible route of approach to what Uncle Trinity had been obsessed by for the past hour. The bell.

'Wow,' said Tamburlaine, reverently. 'It's enormous.'

From where the two mice stood, they had a clear view up into the cup of the bronze. The bell was about nine inches across, green with age, and welded by a short stem onto a square-sectioned rod fixed at either end in a wooden box. The decorative lower supports of this box, like inverted chessmen, reached down very close to the upper rim of the open casement window. From there an athletic mouse would be able to reach up, lash himself on by his tail and climb into the box.

The bell was rung by someone on the ground, far below, a dizzying thirty feet or more, pulling at a long rope. This drew the exterior of the bell against a round clapper on a wire hung from the rod and by dint of jerks and steady tuggings produced a sonorous resonance of the kind the mice had so much objected to.

'It won't be easy,' said Tamburlaine, remembering what Uncle Trinity had suggested to him.

'But possible,' urged Uncle Trinity. 'Undoubtedly possible.'

It was true. The plan was simple. The mice would climb up through the casement and into the box. They would each take one end of the bell's supporting rod and gnaw away at the surrounding wood. Working gradually, they would nibble a complete ring round one side, and a partial ring round the other.

All this could be done while straddling the rod, holding on by their tails. Towards the end, however, when the rod was loosening and ready to break away, they would have to gnaw footholds in the side wall of the box and finish the demolition work from there.

One end would eventually rip away, and they would then climb round the side of the box and gnaw at the other side, from above, until it too gave, and the great bell was sent thundering down to a smashing encounter with the flagstones of the pathway outside the back door. The whole process would be very similar to that

used many a time by Uncle Trinity in the fields to fell a
sapling or a stalk of corn. He knew exactly where to
make the tooth-marks, how deep to penetrate and when
the sapling would be ready to give.

'The only difficulty,' he had said to Tamburlaine as he
outlined his plan for the bell-felling, 'will be the height.
We'll be working further from the ground than usual.
Otherwise, it will all be normal practice.'

Now a chill wind came through the window with a
hint of rain in it, and Tamburlaine shivered. He
remembered something his mother had told him when
he used to shiver at home.

'Somebody's walking over your grave,' she had said.

24
Inside the Box

'Let's do it now,' said Uncle Trinity suddenly.

Tamburlaine stared at him.

'But you said we'd just do a reconnaissance,' he objected. 'Surely we ought to tell the others first.'

'Not really,' said Uncle Trinity plausibly.

He felt a great need to get on and do the job. The window was open, nobody was there. The time was ripe.

'It only takes two pairs of teeth,' he said. 'The rest would just be in the way. They'd be looking on. We can do it best ourselves, young Tamburlaine.'

Tamburlaine stared up again at the bell. It seemed to swing slightly in its box, at once threatening and inviting.

'Just you and I,' said Uncle Trinity. 'We'll be heroes afterwards. The mice who broke the bell.'

Inside his head, Tamburlaine felt his tune start. He puffed out his chest and bristled his whiskers.

'Great mice have been before me,' he hummed. 'Great mice are still to come.'

'Come on,' said Uncle Trinity. 'Give me a paw.'

Already he was on the bottom rim of the casement, the wind catching and ruffling his grey fur.

'All right,' said Tamburlaine.

He took a grip on the metal rim and swung out and up. Far below, as he glanced briefly down, he could see the evergreen of the laurel and the dead keys on the laburnum: a little nearer, but still a huge distance off it seemed, there sloped the grey tiles of the dairy roof.

Tamburlaine averted his eyes. Like all field mice, he had no fear of heights, but he was aware of how important it was going to be not to lose his footing.

'From here,' Uncle Trinity was saying, looking up, 'we try to coil our tails on the catch and then use our claws to bring up our whole weight. You see that metal bar, above the first row of leaded lights? We can make a swing from that.'

There was no doubt about it, thought Tamburlaine. Uncle Trinity was amazingly acrobatic when it came to working at heights. His weight seemed to melt away and he almost floated onto the window-catch, as if he was a kind of portly balloon and not a solid ball of flesh.

Tamburlaine gritted his teeth. He wasn't going to be outdone by an old mouse twice his age. With a slight jump he reached and held the metal bar, dangling for a moment to feel the grip. Then he used all the strength in his forepaws and swung sideways until his long tail could flick and find a hold on the arc of the catch. Once he got one, it was easy. As he'd done many times before in the fields he pulled his whole weight up on his tail.

'Very good,' said Uncle Trinity in his ear. 'Now here I want you to make me a back while I scramble onto the upper rim of the window. I know I'm heavy but you'll hardly feel my weight I'll move so fast. When I'm up I'll reach down and give you a paw.'

Tamburlaine did as he was told. It was athletic but satisfying work, and he felt a great confidence in the obvious experience and skill of his uncle. In a few moments, the two mice were squatting on the hinge by the wall, studying the approach to the last stage of their climb, the way into and up the wooden box.

As Tamburlaine leaned against the loose cement where the brickwork of the wall needed repointing, he felt a gust of wind sweep by. There were clouds running in the sky now and the first drops of what might be a storm were falling.

'We'll be well sheltered inside the box,' said Uncle Trinity, reading his thoughts. 'Neither the wind nor the rain will bother us there.'

Tamburlaine nodded. He hoped not. He watched as Uncle Trinity coiled his tail and clambered up near to the dependent moulding of the box. It was rather like, he thought, the swirling tip of an ice cream. There was one at each of the four corners and the box, if inverted, would have presented something of the aspect of a toy castle or a sort of wooden crown.

'Follow me,' said Uncle Trinity, and before Tamburlaine could have counted five he was out and up and peering down from above, a neat, familiar, cheerful face, balanced in the moulding and supported on a strong tail coiled round the bell's long bar.

The distance was actually very small and Tamburlaine found that he could lean over from the rim of the window and get a grip with his paws. After that, the swing up and round with his tail was easy.

Breathing hard, and feeling the white painted wood of the box round him like a little house, Tamburlaine felt safer and more prepared for the gnawing work ahead.

'You're doing well,' said Uncle Trinity, patting his

shoulder. 'From now on it's just the hard grind, I'm afraid. I'll take this end of the rod here and I want you to swing over and make a start on the other side. But remember: you're only to gnaw at the wood from above the bar.'

There was a pattering sound and a fierce swish of wind. The rain had started and was blowing in gusts against the outside of the box. It suddenly felt snug and warm inside.

'If you get the least sign of loosening or hear a creak or feel a strain, stop gnawing at once and call me over,' said Uncle Trinity.

Tamburlaine nodded. Then, with a long swing, he brought himself onto the bar and crawled along until he could straddle the metal comfortably. The great hill of green bronze that formed the bell soared away below in a sweeping curve. Beside him, and providing a fine support for his back, there was the iron ball of the clapper, attached to the bar by a strip of wire. It felt chill against his fur, but it was good to lean on.

He looked back over his shoulder. There was Uncle Trinity, resting his bulk on the right-angle bar from which the bell-rope went fraying down, down and down and down and down, thought Tamburlaine, all that distance right to the back door, where the chambermaid normally stood to pull it.

Tamburlaine shuddered. He was rather glad he was working at this side where he couldn't see to the ground. Uncle Trinity had been thoughtful to arrange that.

There was a sound of crunching, a steady whirring sort of grinding noise, like a saw working. It was Uncle Trinity, gnawing already in a regular circle around the bar. Tamburlaine sniffed the air. There was a dank, mouldy smell, dry rot perhaps in the wood. It ought to be easy chewing if that were so.

Revenge, thought Tamburlaine. We'll teach them to smoke us out of our homes. They'll learn their lesson.

But he didn't feel revengeful. After all, nothing had really happened yet. More than revenge he felt a sense of adventure, of taking part in a ritual test of mousehood. He began to gnaw.

As he gnawed, something strange happened. He began to remember Caesar, his dead brother who had sacrificed his life for the family and Tamburlaine began to hum. 'Great mice have been before me. Great mice are still to come.'

As he gnawed at the other end of the rod, Uncle Trinity heard him and smiled. His own rage and bitterness had all been dissolved into the energy of planning, and now he gnawed with a rare vigour, entirely absorbed in the nicety of the bell-felling. It had

become a precise operation for Uncle Trinity, a matter of placing the tooth-marks right. Vengeance was in the wings, an incidental benefit.

It was then, with the wood half chewed through at each end and minutes of gnawing still to do, that Humbleside released his canisters of poison smoke in the cellar, watching the blue spirals curl and forage under stone wine bins and through crannies in barrels and storage crates, killing whatever life was there to be killed, winter spiders and wood beetles, a few early pond flies, and a wealth of woodlice and mites. They died choking and, if they had eyes, with eyes watering, as the men gassed on the battlefields of Loos died and for no better reason.

'In half an hour or so,' Humbleside had said as he addressed the assembled household in the kitchen, after the bell had rung, and been heard by Uncle Trinity and Tamburlaine and Gioconda in the rafters, and by all the other mice wherever they were on their patrols, 'I shall lay my poison smoke in the cellar. To give you all an exact warning, Mary will ring the bell a second time.'

So now, with the smoke at its lethal work and the two mice in the fortress of the bell, the chambermaid wiped her hands on her apron at the laundry room sink, went outdoors and took a firm grip on the dangling rope, giving it a steady and then a jerking pull.

It was the jerking pull that brought the iron clapper up and then down on Tamburlaine's back.

'Look out,' Uncle Trinity had called as soon as he felt the square-sectioned bar turn and squirm under his legs. 'They're ringing the bell again.'

But the warning had come too late. For Tamburlaine, with his teeth in the wood and his mind on glory, the turn in the bar meant nothing more than a shift in his own position. He didn't realize until too late that the clapper was moving against his fur.

The body of Tamburlaine went down like a spinning plummet, over and over, a grey blur under Uncle Trinity's helpless eyes, until it hit the slant of the dairy roof, and then bounced on the tiles, and then rolled, head over heels, and came to rest in the gutter.

25
Effects of the Smoke

There was no hope already, Uncle Trinity knew that, even as he swung down and found a grip on the moulding, and then the window frame, and was going down it on all fours, flat out, as fast as he could run.

But surely, he thought, as he raced across the floor and down the flight of stairs, and then the second flight, and into the sewing room. Surely there was always hope.

He reached the wall under the scrap-paper screen, covered with politicians in beards and glasses and fine ladies with parasols, and from there dug under the skirting board and found the hole and was up, scrambling now and breathless, a fat old sorrowful mouse again, who had done something stupid he'd have to regret for the rest of his life, no more a fine warrior, no more a great soldier with a brave young captain to carry out his orders.

'Tamburlaine,' called Uncle Trinity, across the cold roof, feeling the sleet dashed like tears in his face now. 'Tamburlaine, are you all right?'

But there was no reply from the crumpled heap of grey fur, out there with its head in soaking leaves.

Tamburlaine, young Tamburlaine, the flower of chivalry, the apple of his father's eye, the last of his line, was dead.

Uncle Trinity stood above him now in the biting wind, knowing the worst. He felt the earlier violence drain away from his mind and a slow, trickling grief replace it, sadness and a terrible bitter sense of guilt and shame.

But there was no time for emotion. Uncle Trinity looked right and left along the gutter and then down over the edge to the muddy path below that went round the apple store to the chestnut tree. Any moment now, as often in this part of the garden, the padding relentless shapes of the cats might appear, questing and prowling for something to chase and kill.

The dairy roof was one of their favourite hunting grounds. They had an easy way up from a rain barrel outside the coal-store and from there to the slates and the ridge line. Very many young tits in spring had breathed their last in an unguarded second spent idly preening or gossiping on the dairy roof.

Now it was icy cold and swept by the sleety rain in long sudden gusts from the east. Uncle Trinity shivered. It was fearsome weather to do what he had to do in, but at least it offered some chance of making progress while the cats still lurked indoors and kept warm.

From the owls there was nothing to fear, at least for Tamburlaine. They were only interested in living creatures, thought Uncle Trinity grimly, and poor Tamburlaine was no longer one of those. He had gone to where his brother Caesar was, to some mouse haven beyond the reach of storm or claw. Only his mortal remains were left.

It was these mortal remains that immediately concerned Uncle Trinity. For the mice death was a common event, and they accepted the severance of consciousness with stoicism. The proper disposal of bodies, however, was something that they all felt strongly about, not least because of the frequency with which their bones were eaten, or thrown in rubbish, or burnt away.

It was a point of pride with Uncle Trinity, as it would have been with any mouse, to try and remove the body of Tamburlaine from its exposed position, and to see that it was kept safe until such time as there could be a decent burial.

This duty took precedence over the reconciliation of his warring feelings, and even over the preservation of his life. It was hard for Uncle Trinity to put his emotions aside and concentrate on a plan. But he had to do it.

On the slippery roof, with the wind rushing and pausing in irregular gusts, it was going to be risky to try and move the body of Tamburlaine on his own, but Uncle Trinity decided that there wasn't time to go and look for help. He had to make a beginning at once.

Reaching under Tamburlaine's forepaws, Uncle Trinity took the weight of his body against his own ample belly. Wheezing with effort, he began to back slowly towards the hole through which he could find his way to the sewing room.

Tamburlaine's forefeet dragged in the mess of sodden leaves in the gutter. More than once Uncle Trinity had to stop and put him down while he cleared a path with his claws. All the time the wind hissed and whistled in a derisory paean.

Gasping and breathless, Uncle Trinity managed to pull the body to the corner of the house. There he rested

a moment, watching the high clouds scudding above
the beeches, and trying to forget what it was he was
carrying.

Through the shrubbery, where the rose of Sharon
had flowered almost until Christmas, there were
puddles gathering and ridges of soft mud. Any one of
these would have been deep enough for Uncle Trinity to
sink and drown in.

Uncle Trinity shook himself and made a final effort.
Head first, he went through the hole in the plaster and
jumped down onto the plank floor. Then he reached up
and out and lifted the body of Tamburlaine onto his
shoulders. Gradually, backing away in the dim light, he
lowered his dead nephew to the floor.

There Tamburlaine lay, his limbs curled in the foetus
shape they had had when he first waited for life in his
mother, his fur dripping and wet, though not now with
the amniotic fluid, but with the bitter evening rain.

Uncle Trinity left him and ran for the door. Now was

the time to find help. The body of Tamburlaine would
be safe behind the skirting board until the other mice
could arrive to give a hand with its proper removal to
the attic or the garden.

Uncle Trinity climbed the curling flight of stairs and
then the next one, in semidarkness now, to the doorway
of the chambermaid's bedroom. Under the enormous
arch of the architrave, he paused, sniffing. Something
was wrong, very wrong.

A few feet away, at the edge of the carpet, Uncle
Trinity could see an indistinct shape on the dark stain of
the wood. He edged towards it, nose alert, whiskers
twitching. Then he stepped back, retching.

It was a pool of vomit. Worse, it was a pool of cat
vomit. Uncle Trinity, like other mice, had a highly
discriminatory pair of nostrils, and he knew the smell of
different kinds of sickness. One of the cats had been
here, and recently, and was very ill.

From the dark green cupboard that housed the water
tanks, there came a sudden sound. Uncle Trinity
crouched, listening. The room was empty. The maid
was away somewhere, about her business.

There it was again. A sort of convulsive choking
sound, very definitely from behind the cupboard wall.
Uncle Trinity waited one second more, whiskers
bristling. No, he decided, there was no question of it
being a water noise. The tanks might gurgle and wheeze
and even groan and moan, but they never sounded as if
they were scarcely able to breathe.

Uncle Trinity moved fast. The pool of vomit and the
choking sound meant only one thing. A cat, and a very
sick one, was in the tank cupboard.

Skirting another pool of vomit by the chest of
drawers, Uncle Trinity crept across the floor and

through the hole into the cupboard. The sweating bulk of the first tank was by his side, a steely elephant's leg in the darkness.

Pushing his nose round this to where a thin beam of light filtered in from a crack in the boarding, Uncle Trinity saw what had happened.

The Black Prince lay back against a splinter of wood, her lungs heaving in a strange rhythm. Even as Uncle Trinity watched, her body seemed to contort. Uncle Trinity shuddered. So here was the first casualty of the poison. By a dreadful boomerang of retribution, the laying of the smoke had claimed as its first victim one of the rector's own pets.

Uncle Trinity leaned back on the water tank, watching the helpless cat as it struggled for breath only a few feet away from him. Inside his head, he felt a sudden spurt of exhilaration, a sense of pure, appropriate vengeance.

Then the cat's eye rolled in its head and seemed to quiver towards him, blind in its pain, then, almost, as it were, beseeching its former enemy for the help he had no power to give. Uncle Trinity felt a new emotion take root in his heart.

He turned away, a lump in his throat. It was wrong that any animal should have to die like this. Without friends, without aid.

At least Tamburlaine's death had been quick. This prolonged foulness was something else. A kind of punishment not even a cat deserved.

Uncle Trinity turned away and bent his steps towards the rafters.

26
The Burial Party

By the door of the potting-shed, Humbleside paused. He looked up at the sky. The rain had stopped and a thin strip of blue was visible along the horizon.

'We'll have good weather tomorrow,' said Humbleside to Katrine, as she prowled at his ankles.

He laid his mask on the shelf, beside trays of bulbs and a litter of pots and rubber gloves and drying seeds. He had thrown the empty canisters of poison in the fluted dustbin and there they would lie as an awful warning to scavengers until removed by the dustmen on the following Friday.

'A good job well done,' said Humbleside, that unctuous man, as he walked with the cat at his heels through the tangled weedy growth of the old vegetable garden. He slashed at a dead potato-stalk with his stick and felt satisfied. Sufficient unto the day the pollution thereof.

Uncle Trinity's tale had soon been told. He spoke

briefly, but he left nothing out, neither the death of Tamburlaine nor his own responsibility, nor the dying body of the Black Prince in the tank room.

'I'm sorry,' said Uncle Trinity. 'I'm so sorry.'

Amelia Mouse, as was to be expected, had taken the news worst. Although she had always been the one to want something done about the bell, she was quick to accuse Uncle Trinity of indulging his own impetuous nature.

'You ought to have asked us first,' she said. 'My God, you knew that.'

Maternal grief began to sway her sense of reason. 'You killed my son,' she insisted. 'You killed him as surely as if you put your teeth in his neck. And for what? For a pitiable silly need for revenge before anything had happened to justify it.'

'It seemed like a good idea,' Uncle Trinity objected. 'The time was right. After all, we nearly gnawed it through. In another minute we would have done. He died a hero, Amelia. He really did.'

'A hero,' said Amelia Mouse with complete scorn. 'You mean a sacrifice. A sacrifice to your own stupidity.'

'Amelia,' said Grandfather Mouse, raising his paw. 'Please.'

He looked round at the angry and grief-stricken faces of his family. Only a few weeks ago they had been unified by adversity, at one in their aims and actions. The threat of extinction had knit them together, stiffened their mutual allegiance. Now it was crumbling. The fingers of strife were at work in the rafters. War had set mouse against mouse.

'We are one family,' said Grandfather Mouse. 'Remember that. It's true,' he continued with measured judgement, 'that Trinity was in the wrong. He's admitted that. We ought to have made our common decision about the poison and the bell, before any steps were taken.'

'It's all right, Trinity,' said Michaelmas breaking in.

He'd been quite silent until now, but he knew how desperate Trinity was for his forgiveness.

'It's all right,' he repeated more quietly.

Uncle Trinity put his head in his paws. He could say nothing.

'We must see that Tamburlaine has a proper burial,' said Grandfather Mouse, anxious to regain the initiative. 'It's a question of where it has to be.'

Michaelmas had risen to his feet. He walked to the tin support at the door and gazed out along the lines of joists that had been their common home for so long.

'Outdoors, of course,' he said. 'At one time I'd like him to have lain in the harvest field, where the other mice all are. But there's no corn now to cover him.'

He turned and looked back at Amelia, his face drawn with grief.

'We'll put him down in the wood,' he said. 'Under the holm-oak. Near to the mound. It seems the right place in a war, dark and quiet.'

Uncle Trinity lifted his head.

'It's a long way to go, Michaelmas,' he said. 'We'll have to sleep the night outdoors. Unless we want to take a risk on Humbleside not smoking out the rafters.'

Grandfather Mouse nodded.

'We'll certainly have to sleep a night outdoors,' he said. 'It wouldn't do to wake with the smoke already curling through. From what you say about the cat, Trinity, it sounds totally lethal.'

Uncle Trinity shivered, remembering the pool of vomit and the rolling of the Black Prince's eyes.

'Let's go,' he said.

He was fidgety, worried about the body of Tamburlaine, alone there behind the skirting board in the sewing room.

So the three male mice set off on their errand of respect, leaving the female mice behind.

'We'll be quite some time,' said Michaelmas. 'Remember, you're not to go out, or anywhere near the door even. Take care.'

On the way down, there was a curious restraint amongst the mice. Uncle Trinity felt the misery of his guilt seep up and lap around his lungs, making him wheeze and groan and move slowly, weighed under as if by his years. By contrast, the much older Grandfather Mouse was brisk and spry but rather testy and awkward. He realized that the crisis had finally brought his son Michaelmas to the head of the family, and he had to accept this change, and yield to it with grace. Michaelmas himself felt a heavy burden of responsibility. Already his son was dead. But there might be as bad or even worse to come. To prevent himself from brooding, he kept up a flow of conversation about their plans.

'We'll sleep in the earth closet,' he said as they traversed the rafters. 'No one will use it after dark and we'll leave it as soon as the bell goes, at dawn. We'll be warm enough there and safe for one night at least.'

'I imagine you'll want to put Tamburlaine there,' said Grandfather Mouse, 'and move him out in the morning.'

They were all thinking about the little body they were soon to have to lift and mousehandle down the house through passage and chimney, corridor and open space, moving with a decent slowness and yet with speedy circumspection. In the earth closet someone would watch and stay awake all night long, and all day too, lest any creature, animal or insect, come and attempt to molest or interfere with their dead one.

'Trinity,' said Michaelmas. 'I want you to go over to the barns tonight. Let them all know that Tamburlaine is to have his funeral in the wood at high noon. There are plenty of our people there. I want them all to come.'

'I'll go,' said Uncle Trinity.

By now they had reached the sewing room and, as if by common consent, they all paused a moment. Then Uncle Trinity led the way and they passed through the skirting board and stood round the body of Tamburlaine in a tight respectful circle.

Michaelmas went down on his knees. There were tears now in his eyes.

'O, Tamburlaine,' he said. 'You were all I had.'

27
A Surprise Announcement

That night, as Tamburlaine lay on the scrubbed elm of the earth closet with the blood wiped clean from his head and his crumpled limbs gathered on a bed of bay leaves, the rain stopped and the wind rose: a chill, soughing wind, that blasted the first aconites in their green ruffs on the terrace and pinned down their winter hoods on the coming snowdrops where they lifted their spears in the ditch of the old moat.

It was a melancholy wind, and it made the hearts of the mice falter as they kept watch by their fallen one. There was no sleep for Michaelmas as he thought of the future; nor for Grandfather Mouse as he remembered the past; nor for Uncle Trinity with his guilt, when he came back in the small hours from his errand to the barns; nor for Ermintrude and Gioconda as they attended to Boadicea, restless with a feverish dream; nor for Amelia Mouse, least of all for her as she stroked the fur of her dead son. There was only the morning to wait for and the wind to listen to.

The wind howled and it keened, and it rattled the windows of the rectory. It came from the east, and slid along the drainpipes, and made the broken pane in the study creak and give. It made the rector's wife pause with her ebony brush in the air as she sat at her dressing-table and drew her fingers through the long sweep of her unbound hair.

Only the rector seemed oblivious to the wind, as he stood in his black garters folding his trousers neatly before fitting them under the wooden plates of his trouser-press.

'The wind seems very high tonight,' said the rector's wife, starting to brush again with long, even, vigorous strokes.

'Yes, indeed,' said the rector enthusiastically. 'Yes, indeed.'

His thoughts were elsewhere and he hadn't, as often, heard exactly what his wife was saying. A warm, nodding sort of agreement often served very well in these circumstances he'd found. So he slid the dark cloth of his trousers into position, smoothed it down and laid the upper board on top.

'I hope it doesn't bring any slates down from the carriage house roof,' the rector's wife continued, making a face at herself in the tilted Victorian cheval-glass between her candles.

'God's will,' the rector murmured as he began to tighten the screws in the press. 'The wind bloweth where it listeth.'

The word wind had at last sunk in, and his ears now picked up the background moan behind the more immediate rush and swoosh of his wife's hairbrush and the perpetual, steady ticking of the old marble clock on the mantelshelf.

'We ought to get Humbleside to renew the nails,' the rector's wife was saying. 'I'm sure there's rust. It's years since they were done.'

The rector bent and slid his trouser-press underneath the bed where it lay beside leather suitcases, shrouded in dust, and a wooden box with a crochet set that Esmeralda had refused to find a use for after her last birthday.

'Humbleside may have to go to the war,' he said. 'If things continue as badly as they are doing Lloyd George may demand a general call to the colours.'

The rector pulled his vest over his head and shook his nightshirt onto his shoulders. Leaning back on the turned sheets, he unclipped his garters and drew off his socks.

'I wonder if we really ought to be bothering about the attic,' the rector's wife said, turning on her stool by the window. 'Surely the carriage house roof is more important. And if Humbleside has to go and fight the Germans, we'd better use him while we can.'

'I've asked Mary to clear the rafters out tomorrow,' the rector said. 'We could use the space for Monty and Gorgo to play in.'

Outside the window the gale rose in a sudden shrill wail, and there was a clatter of something falling somewhere.

The rector closed his eyes.

'Let's go to sleep, my dear,' he said.

Alas, it was a short sleep, if perhaps an easy one. But the rector's awakening was far from easy. His eyes opened under the stress of a fierce shaking and he sat up suddenly, bolt upright on the pillow, staring startled into the tear-stained face of his wife, flickeringly illuminated by the light of a guttering candle pinned in a brass holder.

'Simon,' his wife was saying. 'Wake up, Simon. Something awful has happened.'

The rector, ever ready for whatever domestic calamity might need his attention, was at once over the side of the bed and reaching for his spectacles.

'One moment, my dear,' he said as he hastily attempted to find his slippers. 'One moment and I shall attend to you.'

He looked sleepily about him, searching for signs of his dressing-gown. In the dim glow of the candle flame, he observed the chambermaid, hovering awkwardly in the bedroom doorway.

'Why, Mary,' he said, in some embarrassment. 'Forgive me. I didn't see that you were there.'

The rector rapidly drew the dressing-gown round his shoulders, and poked his arms through the sleeves. Thus dressed, he felt better and more able to cope with whatever trouble – fire or flood or German parachutist – had occurred to mar the decent order of his household.

He peered more closely at the chambermaid, seeing that she, like his wife, had been crying.

'Why, Mary,' he said more kindly. 'What is it, my girl? Tell me what the matter is.'

But it was the rector's wife, a buxom whirlwind of sudden grief and prostration, who bore him back in her arms onto the bed, sobbing and distraught.

The rector took the candle from her loosening fingers and set it in safety onto the floor before leaning over to smooth her hair and comfort her distress.

The tall flame, caught in a draught from the door, wavered and nearly went out, then gathered strength and sent a weird, unearthly light on their faces as they lay together.

'That stupid Humbleside,' the rector's wife exclaimed. 'I knew we should never have let him use his foul smoke in the first place. But you were so sure, Simon. Oh, you were so very sure!'

The rector's brow furrowed. He was at a loss to know exactly what had happened. He patted his wife's cheek, and leaned round on his elbow, addressing Mary where she still stood in shadow beside the door.

'Mary, my dear,' he said as calmly as he could. 'Whatever has happened to distress you both so much? In the name of God, I ask you to tell me what has happened.'

The chambermaid came forward into the light of the candle, her feet sloughing on the bare boards. She clutched her thin nightgown tightly round her shoulders.

'Oh, sir,' she said. 'I scarcely know what to say. It were that awful when I kneeled down to say me prayers, and there she was. Oh, sir.'

A fit of snivelling obstructed any further advance of this narrative, and the rector was left unsatisfied and no wiser for the moment than before.

'I see that you are most upset,' he said firmly, rising from the bed and taking a pace across the carpet. 'I must ask you, however, to take a grip on yourself. Your mistress is quite beside herself with grief and I must know the cause of this at once.'

The rector paused.

'I shall say a brief prayer,' he said with his full religious calm, 'and then I shall expect to hear a coherent account of what has taken place. Our Father.'

The maid kneeled down and placed her head between her hands on the coverlet of the bed. The rector's wife lay quietly moaning and clasping her fingers in her mouth. Outside the wind howled, as it had done all evening, and along the floor the candle-flame flickered like the fires of hell.

But the steady rhythm of the rector's voice as he went through a gentle prayer for consolation in distress was enough to restore a little order to the shattered nerves of the two women, and by the time that he had finished Mary was able to wipe her tears and try to tell her tale.

'I told the mistress,' she said with a gulp. 'I knelt down to say my prayers like I always do at night, sir, and I felt a sort of tickling against my knee, as if a corner of the rug had curled up.'

There was a sudden louder rush of wind and the candle flame guttered, brightened, then went completely out.

'One moment,' the rector said and in black darkness

he fumbled in the chest of drawers for the spare candle that was always kept there. It took longer to find a match, to shield it against the wind and to get the new candle to light. But at last it did, and the room was again vaguely illuminated as Mary continued her story.

'It weren't the rug,' the maid said, her face turned up, wide-eyed, toward the rector. 'It were 'er. Poor little thing. Poor little thing.'

A paroxysm of weeping again struck the maid and she covered her face in her hands.

'In Heaven's name,' said the rector somewhat testily now. 'Who, my dear? Who?'

'Your wretched creature Humbleside,' the rector's wife cried out, half rising from the bed, her face streaked with tears. 'That's who it was. Who else, indeed?'

At this moment the maid recovered a little and managed to reach the end of her tale.

'Sir,' she said more quietly. 'I put out me hand, to see what it was like, and I felt the smoothness of her fur. I thought at first she'd come upstairs to say goodnight, like she sometimes do, and I stroked her back and spoke to her, saying her name. "There now, Black Prince," I said. "There you are, my fine girl." But she felt very still somehow. Very unresponsive to my fingers.'

The maid's voice made a quiet low foreground to the rising howl of the wind. The rector leaned beside his wife, gently stroking her hair and patting her forehead as he listened.

'Then I got up and lit a candle, sir,' the maid said. 'I'd been in the dark, you see. So I held up the candle and then there she were. Stretched out dead on the board, sir, like a rabbit for a dog's dinner.'

There was a long silence. The rector could feel his wife's breast heaving under his arm. He felt a pang go through him. Cats were not his favourite animals but he knew that his wife had idolized the Black Prince.

'I take it the body is still there,' he said and then, receiving a nod from Mary by way of affirmative, he went on. 'Stay here, my dear. I shall go with Mary to see what can be done.'

The rector drew the covers over his wife, kissed her on the forehead and, lifting the candle in one hand, put his other under Mary's chubby elbow and guided the girl through the door and down the corridor towards her bedroom.

There, in front of the chest of drawers, four feet below the open family bible, her long furry legs rigid and folded together, the Black Prince lay in her death, the first victim of the terrible smoke that Humbleside had let loose that morning through the cellars.

She lay with her face out of sight, half under the leg of the chest and it was not until the rector bent and gingerly drew the body out into the light of the candle that the full horror of her expression could be seen.

'Stand back, Mary,' the rector said. 'I don't want you to look at this, my dear.'

The cat's eyes were protruding like marbles from their sockets. There had been no air to breathe, the cat's death had been a hard and cruel one.

The rector got to his feet. He stood for a moment, thinking. Then he turned to Mary.

'Get dressed,' he said. 'Then go down to the carriage house and wake Barker. I want him to go into the village and summon Humbleside. I need to see him at once. Tonight.'

28
The Maid in the Morning

It was the bell that woke Michaelmas in the morning. Tolling with all its old insolence and sombre warning, interrupting the dawn chorus of thrush and sparrow with a more peremptory note, a more clamorous and human cadence.

A challenge and a threat it seemed to Uncle Trinity, as he stood his watch over Tamburlaine's body in a heap of straw, remembering his idle boast that the bell would never ring again. Uncle Trinity frowned in his grief, knowing the insidious pull for vengeance once more in his heart.

After midnight, the mice had decided to take it in turns to watch with Tamburlaine. As a species they needed sleep, and it would do no good to anyone if they started to nod and doze in the solemn process of the funeral. So Amelia had sat up first, as was her mother's right, then Ermintrude and then Michaelmas. Gioconda was sleeping, with Boadicea.

The sun was already inching its crimson gong above the horizon towards the ruined church at Billockby when Uncle Trinity felt his brother's paw on his shoulder and woke, rubbing his eyes, to take his turn. Despite the lateness of the hour Michaelmas had lain down in the straw under the planed side of the earth-box, determined to catch what little rest he could. It was going to be a long and wearisome day.

In a few seconds he'd been in dreamland, aware by some merciful providence only of the harvest-field in the springtime, with a flurry of martins diving over his old house in the corn and the stiff spurt of a skylark spraying his ears with its fountain of sound.

It was so for a time, until the bell clanged, rough and abusive at the end of its frosted rope in Mary's chilblained hands, the long notes tumbling and rising with a different sense of purpose today, as the mice waited in the earth closet to pay their last respects to the dead.

They were like the solemn clangour of a funeral march in the wakeful ears of Amelia Mouse, weeping beside her son: like the jeering rancour of a Roman triumph for a foreign slave led in chains, to the quickening bitterness of Uncle Trinity: like a distant echo from a world he would never see again to the aching bones of Grandfather Mouse, after a night spent trying to sleep on unfamiliar stone.

But to Michaelmas, in his dream, as the harvest-field receded in a bloody mist of scythes, the remote, slavering bell was the herald of nightmare, the intrusive messenger from that future world of hard planning and grim travel he had to wake and prepare his family for.

'Curse them,' he heard Uncle Trinity say as he came awake and stretched to his feet. 'We ought to have finished the job. It's as if they're crowing over us.'

'Give it time, Trinity,' said Grandfather Mouse. 'Don't blame yourself.'

Michaelmas went over to look at Boadicea. She was resting in a warm nest of cotton wool. Through a tiny slit in the door of the earth closet a ray of sun was creeping in. It made a wall of light, fluttering with motes of dust. To his right, as the bell's tolling dwindled and shivered into a tinkling silence, the bulk of the rectory loomed grey as a border keep in the wan morning sun. It was frosty still, and the dead oak leaves on the cobbles crinkled as Michaelmas turned and scampered around under the dead willow.

Very soon Fritz Keitel would be arriving in his khaki van from the camp at Caister, whistling his way to the side door, and perhaps the boy from the village too, replete with porridge and honey, and ready, maybe, to waste a few idle minutes in the earth closet on his way to the dairy. The mice would be safe enough, hidden in the straw on the floor, but they ought to make a move for the wood as soon as they could.

Michaelmas knew this, but he needed a few minutes on his own, a quiet walk in the cold air to straighten his mind and stiffen his will. He turned the corner of the sheds, moving along level with the road now, to the north of the house where the ground was iron-hard and white underfoot.

A blackbird swooped past, shadowing Michaelmas with its wing for a moment as it prowled for bread. There were no worms at this season, but the cook still threw some shreds of old rolls on the coalhouse roof.

Lucky you, thought Michaelmas.

Mice might be vermin but birds were still safe. Even the savage Humbleside would have drawn the line at stoning a cuckoo. As for those prattling blue-tits, and the great conceited robin and his wife, they were protected species.

Michaelmas paused at the corner of the apple-store wall. As he did so, he congratulated himself on his caution. The side door was opening as he glanced to his left and the chambermaid was emerging with a basketful of rubbish to throw in the bins by the gate.

Michaelmas watched her. She was a plump, nimble girl, a bit like Uncle Trinity in her way, thought Michaelmas, and she moved with a sprightly grace in her starched apron and polished lace-up boots. Something tumbled from her arms and Michaelmas watched her stoop to lift the bin lid.

'Mary,' a voice called suddenly from the house. 'Come here, will you?'

It was the voice of the rector, up with the lark for once and requiring some early morning service, a log for his fire or a jug of milk for his tea. The chambermaid laid her basket on the ground and scuttled for the door, wiping her hands on her dress. At this time of day the rector was never in the best of tempers, and it didn't pay to keep him waiting.

Michaelmas watched her go indoors and then ran forward to the bins. There might be something he could use for the burial, some scrap of wood or linen.

There might have been, but there wasn't. Upside down in the root of the tree, with its lid torn from its hinges, was a long wooden cigar-box, the torn label marked Carl Upmann, 25 Coronas. Michaelmas walked slowly round the bin. On the other side, heaped up in the laundry basket the chambermaid had left lying on the ground, was a pile of other boxes, some made of wood, some of cardboard, and there in the middle, a dented silvery Crawford's biscuit tin, with a picture on the side of Queen Victoria at Balmoral.

The attics had been cleared.

29
One Blind Mouse

It was raining again, a thin drizzle at high noon. The mice were gathered in a small circle at the foot of the twisting holm-oak, in the heart of the rector's wood. There was a quiet sound of dripping all round them, mingled with the occasional dull hiss of the wind and the scuffing of their feet.

The journey from the earth closet had lasted for several hours and the mice were tired. The body of Tamburlaine had been washed in rainwater and arranged on a single stiff leaf of laurel, flecked with yellow and shaped like a narrow shield. The older mice had taken it in turns to carry the bier, two at a time, with a third helping to negotiate the burden over obstacles.

Gioconda had been left behind to look after Boadicea, who was too feverish to travel, at least until the mice knew where they were going. So the older female mice were also free to help with the body. Nevertheless, it had been an exhausting, and a perilous, journey.

They had carried Tamburlaine under the ash tree and across the lawn in full sight of the kitchen windows; they had lifted his body through the forest of snowdrops beside the pond and then down and along under the garden seat below the Portuguese laurel; they had eased their burden over stones and fallen twigs, threading their way through the long swoop of the cotoneaster hedge and past the elm stump that had once been Tamburlaine's castle; they had rested, eating a funeral breakfast of hawthorn berries by the holly tree at the corner of the field; then they had hoisted the leaf again to their shoulders and trudged on through the clumps of bluebell spears in the gnarled roots of the great beech tree that was older than any human settlement on the rector's land; they had changed holds and the two women had borne Tamburlaine on the long but easier stretch beside the iron railings between the field and the lawn; at the edge of the wood, Grandfather Mouse and Michaelmas had again taken over the burden, and Tamburlaine had moved through the twilight world of the dying underbrush, the crackling sucker shoots of winter elm.

Now he lay as he had come, still in his shallow position on the laurel leaf, hooped in the famous mouse curve that was always reserved for the dead. The grave he would lie in under the soaring trunk of the holm-oak was already dug, soil heaped in a tall mound alongside the roots.

Uncle Trinity and Michaelmas had stood side by side and worked with their hindpaws until the hardened earth grew loose; then both had turned and scooped with forepaws and teeth until the looser undersoil had come away to a sufficient depth and length.

Amelia Mouse and Ermintrude had lined the grave with leaves of beech and oak, slate-hard and brown under their wintry fur. The bottom of the grave they filled with bay leaves, the same ones as Tamburlaine had rested on all night in the earth closet.

The falling rain crinkled on the forest floor, a gentle weeping sound in the background as Michaelmas and Amelia Mouse lifted the body of their son and laid him in his last resting place. For a moment they stood back, a little breathless.

Michaelmas glanced round. Away to his right was the gentle rise of the Viking burial mound, with its ring of yews and its view out over the flat land to the Bure, where in summer distant yachts could be seen cutting the even green of the fields. Today the view was barer, a stark tracery of boughs over brown ploughland.

Michaelmas turned. On the other side, the wood ran clear away into the field, then swept and turned for the house, out of sight from here almost, except for an urn at the brink of the terrace. Very soon the rector would be pacing there, as he did winter and summer after his lunch, meditating refinements to his next sermon.

Michaelmas glanced at the circle of mice. Outside the inner ring of his immediate family, grouped at a proper distance, were Ethelred with Dotty and Minx from the barns, all looking a little awkward and uncomfortable; beyond them, in the shadow of the yews, were a few other mice, friends and neighbours who had come to show their respect.

As the soil was thrown down into the grave, each member of the family moving forward to help with forepaw and tooth, one of the strange mice from the yews came over and touched Michaelmas awkwardly on the shoulder. Michaelmas turned, feeling the drizzle on his face, unable to see clearly in the smirr.

The strange mouse was walking with a white twig of

blackthorn which he carried stiffly held out in front of him. His eyes were opaque and staring.

'Dear God,' said Michaelmas. 'You're blind.'

'You don't remember,' said the strange mouse. 'It's been too long.'

But Michaelmas did remember. Reaching out his hands he clasped the strange mouse by the cheeks. They were the same as those he had held once in the cornfield, older now and stronger, but the same familiar flesh and blood.

'Horatius,' whispered Michaelmas. 'My son.'

It was a long story, but it made a shaft of light break like an ambiguous dawn on that sad and final scene by the grave.

Horatius, the younger of their two sons, who had been carried away from Amelia and Michaelmas by the

harvest flood in the ditch; Horatius, who had dis-
appeared as it seemed for ever the night the family had
had to flee from their home in the corn; Horatius,
whose brother Caesar had given his life that night to
save his own from the owl; Horatius, whose name like
his brother's had lingered with Tamburlaine since his
father told him the tale of their exile; Horatius, who had
been cast up blind but alive in the wood, and stumbled
for safety until he reached the barns and survived there
with other mice in the western stable, never knowing
what had happened to his family and fearing they were
all dead; Horatius, who had been looked after by kind
strangers and who had heard on a visit to remote
neighbours of his brother Tamburlaine and his funeral
that very day; Horatius had at last returned to his own.

That day the rector set off shortly before noon for his
regular morning walk in the garden. He took his way, as
he often did, along the curving path from the Gothic
door in the orchard wall towards the great beech tree,
and then on over the leaf-strewn grass down to the
wood.

The rector's thoughts were on the sermon he was
preparing for the following Sunday and his eyes, in
concert with the humble comparisons he was formu-
lating for his high ideals, were fixed a few feet before his
boots. He walked, in fact, head down and was able to
conduct a close observation of the ground.

So it happened that, as the rector passed under the
stripling oaks and then below the beech hedge,
crunching fallen nuts and nut-cases under his soles, he
was aware of a tiny movement in the crinkled fire of the
leaf piles.

The rector stopped. Reaching out with the tip of his

cane, he ferreted for a moment amongst the leaves. There was more movement, and then a tiny snout and a pair of bristling whiskers came into view.

The rector bent, and laid his cane on the ground. Very gently, he reached out and lifted a small, quivering dormouse into his hands.

'God's creature,' he murmured. 'I wonder.'

Then he put the little mouse down and watched it scamper away towards the mound.

The rector watched it go, a puzzled smile creasing his face. He was surprised to see the tiny animal stumble, and then seem to change direction. It didn't quite seem to know where it was going.

'God's creature,' the rector repeated. 'Yes, I suppose it is.'

But it never occurred to him that the little mouse was blind.

Later that day the Black Prince was buried with full human pomp and circumstance in a corner of the fig-tree garden, where the bones of two former dogs already lay installed, under tiny wooden crosses the children had carved and illuminated with burnt inscriptions.

Michaelmas watched from a corner of the empty rafters. He tried to tell his blind son, Horatius, exactly what he was seeing.

'You know,' said Horatius as he listened. 'I think we can live here safely again now, father. I could tell when the rector picked me up in his hands. They were gentle with me. Perhaps there won't be any more poison after all.'

'I wonder,' said Michaelmas. 'Let's hope so.'

He looked round the swept and barren spaces of his former home. There was nothing left of what had once been a little hamlet of mouse houses. But perhaps, with luck and energy, they could still make a new start.

Overseas, the war had still two years to run. Many men were to die, among them Humbleside, exorting his platoon to cross the Sambre canal. But at Oby rectory, in the heart of Norfolk, a beginning had been made. The surge of cruelty had reached its high tide and had begun to ebb. The deaths of Tamburlaine and the Black Prince had not been entirely in vain.

On the following pages you will find details of other exciting books from Sparrow.

IN THE GRIP OF WINTER

Colin Dann

The sequel to the award-winning 'The Animals of Farthing Wood'.

Fox, Kestrel, Badger, Toad, Mole, Adder and a host of other small animals have all helped each other on the perilous journey from their threatened home in Farthing Wood to what they believe to be the safety of the White Deer Nature Reserve. But the animals soon discover that their troubles have only begun. . .

Faced with one of the hardest winters on record and hunted by poachers who have stolen into the reserve, the animals of Farthing Wood must band together once again if they hope to survive.

A PATTERN OF ROSES

K. M. Peyton

'T.R.I. 17 February 1910' were the words written under one of the drawings in the Ingrams new family home, *Inskips*. They were also the initials that fifteen-year-old Tim Ingram found engraved on a mossy tombstone in the local churchyard. The tombstone revealed that T.R.I. had died one month short of his sixteenth birthday. Tim found himself strangely drawn to this mysterious boy who had lived in the same house and had had the same initials as himself. Why had he died so young?

Assisted by his friend Rebecca, Tim set out to find out more about T.R.I. — and found himself involved in an astonishing and dangerous mystery.

'A magnificent new novel' *Daily Telegraph*

THE TEAM

K. M. Peyton

Ruth Hollis has grown too large for her much-loved pony, Fly-by-Night, and needs to find a replacement. At the Marshfield auction Ruth sees a pony she thinks she recognizes. It has a resigned and beaten look now, but she can sense the spirit and strength still there beneath the surface. Impulsively, she buys the pony – and then must face up to what she's done.

Buying the new pony means that Ruth must part with Fly, and then go on to discover whether or not the new chestnut is really the pony for her. As Ruth and her new pony try to become a team, the Area Trials become a testing point for both of them.

THE PRIZE PONY

Josephine Pullein-Thompson

Debbie read her letter again, to make sure she'd made no mistake. 'Mum,' she said at last. 'Mum, read this. I *think* it says I've won first prize. I *think* I've won a pony!'

Winning the story competition seemed like a dream come true for Debbie. At last she would have the one thing she had always wanted: a pony of her very own.

But once she got her new pony home, Debbie realized that she had more than she had bargained for. An inexperienced rider, she was no match for the excitable and spirited five-year-old. Before long Debbie is convinced that the pony is nothing but a disaster. Instead of the lovely rides she had imagined, she seems to spend all her time either falling off Easter, or chasing him up and down muddy lanes. Debbie is just at her wits' end when her mother has an idea . . .

THE PONY SEEKERS

Diana Pullein-Thompson

Lynne and David Fletcher saw a terrible summer looming ahead, a summer in which there would be no riding because their parents could no longer afford to keep ponies for them. But the day is saved when their elder sister, the famous ex-show jumper, Briony Fletcher, decides to enlist their help to set up The Pony Seekers, an agency to supply clients with ponies ideally suited to their needs.

All goes well with the first few ponies, but then things begin to go wrong, and Lynne and David realize they must do something desperate if Briony's enterprise is not to be doomed to failure . . .

Diana Pullein-Thompson is one of the three famous Pullein-Thompson sisters who are among the most successful writers of pony stories in Britain.

THE NO-GOOD PONY

Josephine Pullein-Thompson

It was never going to work. The Brodie children disliked the
Dalton children at first sight. The Daltons were smooth and
elegant, their ponies well schooled and their tack immaculate.
The Brodies always looked a mess, their tack was falling apart
and they did not even have a pony each.

But now that Mr Dalton had married Mrs Brodie, the
children were all going to live together. The holidays would
be ruined, and even riding would not be fun any longer with
the Daltons about . . .

A PONY FOUND

Diana Pullein-Thompson

Lynne, David and Briony Fletcher loved horses, and everything to do with them, more than anything else in the world. That was why they founded the Pony Seekers in the first place. But sometimes the best intentions in the world can't make things go right. In the first twelve months, when Briony was cheated by experienced dealers and Lynne's beloved pony, Candy, fell ill, it seemed that everything was going wrong. And then, a miracle — the Pony Seekers were offered a yard of stables by a wealthy local man, and it seemed that all their problems would be solved.

But Lynne, David and Briony soon discovered that even miracles have snags.

RICHARD BOLITHO – MIDSHIPMAN

Alexander Kent

It is October 1772 and the sixteen-year-old Richard Bolitho waits to join the *Gorgon*, a seventy-four-gun ship of the line.

Britain is at peace with her old enemies France and Spain; but pirates still threaten British trade routes and the slave trade between Africa and the Americas continues to flourish.

The *Gorgon* is ordered to sail to Africa's west coast to show the flag – and to destroy those who challenge the authority of the King's Navy. For Bolitho, and for many of the young, untrained crew, it is to be a testing time as they are pitted against a ruthless enemy.

The Sparrow Bookshop

Sparrow has a whole nestful of exciting books that are available in bookshops or that you can order by post through the Sparrow Bookshop. Just complete the form below and enclose the money due and the books will be sent to you at home.

THE SECRET OF LOST LAKE	Carolyn Keene	95p ☐
THE WINKING RUBY MYSTERY	Carolyn Keene	£1.00 ☐
THE GHOST IN THE GALLERY	Carolyn Keene	£1.00 ☐
STAR TREK SHORT STORIES	William Rotsler	£1.00 ☐
A PONY FOUND	D. Pullein-Thompson	95p ☐
SAVE THE PONIES	J. Pullein-Thompson	£1.00 ☐
A NIGHT ON THUNDER ROCK	Enid Blyton	95p ☐
DRACULA	Bram Stoker	95p ☐

Humour

FUNNIEST JOKE BOOK	Jim Eldridge	£1.00 ☐
BROWNIE JOKE BOOK	Compiled by Brownies	95p ☐
SCHOOL FOR LAUGHS	Peter Eldin	95p ☐
NOT TO BE TAKEN SERIOUSLY	Colin West	£1.00 ☐

And if you would like to hear more about our forthcoming books, write to the address below for the Sparrow News.

SPARROW BOOKS, BOOKSERVICE BY POST, PO BOX 29, DOUGLAS, ISLE OF MAN, BRITISH ISLES.

Please enclose a cheque or postal order made out to Arrow Books Limited for the amount due including 8p per book for postage and packing for orders within the UK and 10p for overseas orders.

Please print clearly

NAME...

ADDRESS ....

....

Whilst every effort is made to keep prices down and popular books in print, Arrow Books cannot guarantee that prices will be the same as those advertised here or that the books will be available.